A Wedding to Die For

T0352230

Also by Adrianne Lee

A Wedding to Die For

ADRIANNE LEE

New York Boston

Copyright © 2015 by Adrianne Lee
Excerpt from *Delectable* copyright © 2013 by Adrianne Lee
Cover design by Elizabeth Turner
Cover copyright © 2015 by Hachette Book Group, Inc.

Forever Yours
Hachette Book Group
1290 Avenue of the Americas
New York, NY 10104
hachettebookgroup.com
twitter.com/foreverromance

First ebook and print on demand edition: May 2015

Forever Yours is an imprint of Grand Central Publishing.
The Forever Yours name and logo are trademarks of Hachette Book Group, Inc.

The publisher is not responsible for websites (or their content) that are not owned by the publisher.

The Hachette Speakers Bureau provides a wide range of authors for speaking events. To find out more, go to www.hachettespeakersbureau.com or call (866) 376-6591.

ISBN 978-1-4555-7417-9 (ebook edition)
ISBN 978-1-4555-8917-3 (print on demand edition)

In loving memory of my kid sister, Paula Christine Pozzi.
I will always remember your infectious laugh
and the fun times we shared. Miss you,
Polliwog.

Acknowledgments

THANK YOU:

Alex Logan—My amazing editor, the universe smiled on me the day we connected. I couldn't ask for anyone better to work with. You smooth the rough edges from my manuscripts, ease my stress when life piles it on, and make me smile more than you know.

Karen Papandrew—My cheerleader. Thank you for being free for a pizza at the spur of the moment, for your honesty and your encouragement.

Brandi Maxwell—For being excited about this series in the planning stages and ever since.

Jami Davenport—For your friendship, your plotting advice, and your eagerness to read this book.

Gail Fortune—My fabulous agent. You are such a blessing.

A Wedding to Die For

Chapter 1

The body came in on the noon tide just as the beach wedding reached a critical moment.

* * *

Three Days Before the Wedding

"Daryl Anne Blessing, you are the most wonderful maid of honor a bride could ask for," sobbed my best friend Meg Reilly.

Tears poured from her eyes like spring runoff from Mount Rainier as Meg collapsed in my arms. I staggered back, almost falling down the steps of the motel cottage, shock rippling through me. *The paramount duty of a maid of honor is to keep the bride emotionally calm.* Until this moment, I thought I was doing that.

Until this moment, I would have agreed with her praise of my maid of honor prowess. My short, black hair and blue eyes—the colors of a dark, calm sea—define my penchant for planning, organizing, and keeping everything on an even keel, and are the perfect foil to Meg's long fiery hair, flashing green eyes, and propensity for spur-of-the-moment chaos.

The sunny May day promised a warm afternoon, but at 7:00 a.m. in this small seaside town on Puget Sound, the temperature hovered around thirty-nine degrees. Meg was barefoot, her robe knee-length. I eased her out of the cold, damp morning air and back into the room that looked like a cheap Vegas wedding suite.

Possible causes for Meg's meltdown ran through my mind as I shut the door. Wedding gown, shoes, veil—ordered, arrived, fitting later today. Check. Bridesmaid's dresses, shoes, jewelry—all distributed. Check. My outfit. Check. Bridal shower—last weekend. Check. Bachelorette party. Tonight. Hmmm. Had the stripper canceled?

No. Wait. Meg said I was *wonderful*. That meant something else. Something…*good*? Then why the waterworks? "What's happened?"

Meg released me, sniffling. "*She's* coming."

If Meg had stabbed me, I would have been less stunned. My heart sank. Of all things good I could imagine happening to, or for, my best friend, *her* coming to the wedding was not one of them. God knows, I had nothing to do with it. I'd tried every argument I could think of to talk Meg out of inviting *her*.

I foresaw nothing but disaster in this news. I couldn't allow that. I had to minimize potential damage, but first I'd need more details, and as long as Meg was sobbing, I wouldn't get any.

My gaze raced around the compact room, my vision bombarded by every possible honeymooning couple's fantasy. Hearts and flowers and linked golden bands. Everywhere. I spied a box of tissues on the nightstand and handed one to Meg. I plastered on a smile. *The maid of honor's number one job is to keep the bride emotionally calm.* That meant keeping my opinion to myself. "Why are you crying? This is happy news, right?"

Meg daubed at her watery, green eyes, shoved her mop of long, red curls from her splotched face, and offered me a wobbly smile. "I know you're afraid she'll hurt me again, but it felt wrong not to invite her. After all, she's my mother."

Who ran out on you and your dad when you were eleven! I was there. I'd witnessed the broken child struggling to understand why her mother didn't want her. I hated that Meg struggled still with that sense of being unwanted that had shaped so many of her life choices.

I lost my dad the same year her mother left, and now a memory swept back. I'd escaped his funeral and its aftermath by stealing away to my favorite spot at the end of the dock. Seagulls cried overhead as though they shared my grief. Meg found me, sat down, and offered me candy and condolences. I'd thanked her, shared a long moment of silence, and then I'd turned to her and said, "You understand, don't you?"

We were at that awkward age, little girls not quite preteens, naïve about so many things. And yet there lurked something in Meg's eyes that was too wise for her years. "You mean 'cause we've both lost a parent? Yeah, it makes us the same."

I'd taken her hand, glad of her friendship, but intent on correcting her perception. "Not exactly the same. Your mom can always come home."

"No," she'd said, dead certainty in the word. "She won't. But if your dad could come back he would. He *loved* you."

She'd been right about her mother. Tanya had never come

home. Never phoned. Never written. But now the bitch was coming to her wedding? My heart wrenched. Even though I wanted to shout down the rafters, my best friend needed me to set aside my animosity and put a positive spin on this. I firmed up my smile, but not one supportive word choked from my constricted throat.

"Every girl wants her mother at her wedding," Meg said, snuffling. "You'd want Susan at yours."

Yes, but I wasn't getting married. I wasn't even dating. And my mom wasn't a lying, cheating, family-deserting bitch on wheels. A widow for fifteen years, my mom still lived with her mother-in-law. My parental units put a premium on loyalty. As did I.

As did Meg.

I sighed inwardly. She needed my support now, not bawled out. I summoned courage. Fortitude. A best friend's twin superpowers at times like these. "As long as you're happy, Meg, I'm happy for you."

"Really?" Her smile was crooked and instantly endearing.

"Pinkie swear." We hooked little fingers as we'd been doing since grade school, then crossed our hearts to seal the deal.

"Now wash those eyes and get dressed, and do your makeup magic on that red nose. My body is craving caffeine and a stack of blueberry pancakes."

She stopped the trek across the cabin toward the bathroom, a look of dread crinkling her face. "Not Cold Feet?"

Cold Feet Café is the best place in town to sit down with a cup of your favorite brew and contemplate whatever needs contemplating. It's also Meg's father's business. I had another sinking feeling. "You didn't tell your dad before you sent the invitation, did you?"

She bit her lower lip, hugging her bathrobe. "I know you said I should, but I thought he'd object."

No shit, Sherlock. I suspected, though, she was mostly worried about hurting his feelings. That also worried me. Finn Reilly was the kind of big, strong guy who gave off the impression he could take on the world without blinking—unless you really looked at him and saw beyond the bluster. His quick smile never quite vanquished a dull pain in his eyes.

I had the niggling feeling something bad was brewing, and it wasn't coffee. "Okay, then, Jitters and a blueberry muffin."

While Meg dressed and fixed her hair and makeup, I sat on the bed lost in thought. It seemed such a short time ago that we'd graduated high school and took off to seek our fortunes in Hollywood. A couple of years in, she'd landed a job on a network sitcom as an assistant makeup artist and suggested they hire me as Key Wardrobe, the person in charge of what the actors wear each episode. Where had the time gone? In three days Meg would be married and—

"What are you ruminating about?" Meg said—all signs of a crying jag abolished by her incredible cosmetic finesse—pulling me back to the moment.

Just thinking how our lives are going to change forever once you say "I do," my friend, but I couldn't say that out loud. "Just thinking how much I really need some caffeine."

She laughed as we stepped outside into the bright sunshine. We both wore jeans and sweatshirts. If this were a TV episode, I would have selected these outfits for "two young women eating at a small-town diner." But there was more to it than dressing appropriately. Meg and I were minor celebrities in the hometown-girls-make-good spirit, one of us even marrying a big-name actor, and it was important not to appear to be putting on airs.

We linked hands as though holding tight to our friendship and started down the street. Meg said, "I'm so glad we're here together."

"To quote Dorothy," I said, "there's no place like home."

That made us both laugh. Our hundred-year-old seaside town, located near Fox Island in Pierce County, had come into existence when logging and fishing were mainstays of Pacific Northwest industry. As their economy flourished, the city founders—strapping young bachelors—commissioned a slew of mail-order brides. So many marriages took place the first year this Washington State town was established, it became known as Weddingville.

And the name stuck.

More recently, the town began to flounder. Income was down across the board. With one exception. Blessing's Bridal, the wedding-wear shop my mom and grandmother run. The city council met and discussed the dire situation and came up with a brilliant idea. Turn Front Street into something akin to an out-let mall—for weddings. A kind of one-stop-wedding-shopping experience, everything a bride, groom, or wedding planner could want in a single setting.

Local shopkeepers embraced the proposal, changing not only their merchandise accordingly, but also their storefronts. Jitters espresso stand became Pre-Wedding Jitters, Trudy's Lingerie became Her Trousseau, Ring's Jewelry became The Ring Bearer, Flora's Flowers became The Flower Girl, and so on. Motels were given honeymoon suite makeovers, some more tacky than others. The old community church and several outdoor locales became wedding ceremony sites.

Yes, there truly is "no place like home."

"Hey, this isn't the way to Jitters. Unless…did it move?"

"It didn't move. But you were right. I need to tell Dad."

My appetite fled. "Are you sure?"

"No, but I'm doing it anyway."

"Alrighty then." We trekked the four blocks downhill to Front Street. "After breakfast let's swing by Trudy's and pick out a couple of lacy bits guaranteed to make yours one hot, sexy honeymoon."

"Let's see how my talk with Dad goes first," Meg said, seeing right through my feeble attempt to keep her calm.

How did one tell the dad she adored that she'd invited the woman who'd run out on them fifteen years ago to her wedding? That the invitation was accepted? I shuddered inwardly. Big Finn Reilly was not going to take this well.

Cold Feet Café came into view. Perched on the waterside of Front Street, it shared the brick facade of many other buildings on this street. Cars angled into the curb, and the large windows revealed occupied booths and tables. "Oh God, Meg, the place is packed."

"It's just the usual breakfast crowd," she said, not sounding worried but biting her bottom lip, a sure tell.

I tried not to imagine the emotional tornado that was about to level this small-town diner. And failed. "Maybe you should put this off until the café is—"

"No way. If I put this off any longer, I'll explode."

If she didn't put this off, Big Finn might explode.

Meg swept inside with me on her heels. A bell over the door announced our arrival, but didn't dent the medium-level chatter, the clatter of silverware on plates, or the confluence of delicious aromas. Several folks offered welcome home greetings and congratulations to Meg, which we responded to in kind.

The decor was a cheery red and white with splashes of chrome. My nervous gaze found Big Finn. He stood behind the counter at the far end, deep in conversation with one of the diners. His crisp apron showed breakfast stains. Taller than most by six inches, he stood out like a red-topped evergreen in a forest of baseball-capped saplings.

I caught Meg's arm. "Maybe you should consider saving your news until he isn't so busy."

She wasn't swayed. "It's rip off the bandage time."

I gulped. A band tightened around my chest. I should go with her, but this was between Meg and her father. It was hard to stay where I was as Meg headed toward Big Finn. I felt like I was witnessing a train wreck in the making, yet unable to prevent it.

Halfway to her dad, Meg was stopped in her tracks by a woman with crayon yellow hair seated in one of the booths. "Oh, Meg, I was hoping to catch you here."

Zelda Love, our local wedding planner, patted a folder on the table that looked more like an overstuffed sandwich with its ingredients about to escape from all sides.

I felt a tug on my sleeve. "Oh, Daryl Anne?"

I glanced down at three women seated in a booth. They were my grandmother's age, her Bunko buddies. Velda Weeks had the flyaway gray hair of a fluffy dog and a grin like the Cheshire Cat about to lure Alice into trouble. "Sit, sit."

She indicated the empty spot beside her. I complied, giving them all a warm smile. "How are you?"

"We're more than a little curious," Jeanette Corn, a throwback to the hippie generation, admitted, her thin face more animated than usual. I swear she'd never cut her long hair or worn a touch of makeup. "We hear Meg is getting married."

I was pretty sure the whole town knew that by now.

"And she didn't invite any of us," Velda said, scowling her disapproval.

"I'm doing the cake," Wanda Perroni, the owner of The Wedding Cakery, an Italian bakery, snipped as though that gave her a one-up on Velda and Jeanette. "The smallest one in many years, I can tell you."

"What we want to know is who is this guy she's marrying? Why is it so hush-hush?" Velda asked.

"He must be someone important is what I say," Wanda said. "From Hollywood. A director or movie star. I'm right, aren't I?"

"I'll bet it's George Clooney," Velda said.

"He's married, Velda," Wanda said. "It's probably that guy who does those *Mission Impossible* movies. I hear he's single and looking."

"Meg can't marry him. She's Catholic," Jeanette said. She sighed and did a pretend swoon. "I hope it's that new James Bond. He's a dreamboat."

"I bet it's someone from TV," Velda said. "Like that sexy Shemar Moore on *Criminal Minds* who's always flirting with that computer whiz Garcia and calling her Baby Girl. Does Meg's fiancé call her Baby Girl?"

I sat in stunned silence. I wasn't happy they knew Meg's fiancé was an actor. We'd tried hard to keep that under wraps, but I admired their attempts to get me to spill the beans. TMZ had nothing on the gossips in this town. "Ladies, I can't tell you anything. I've been sworn to secrecy."

"I always thought Meg would marry Troy," Jeanette said. Her friends agreed.

I needed to make an escape without more questions and without offending my gram's friends. But how?

"Does Troy know Meg's getting married?" Velda asked.

Behind me, the doorbell tinkled, and a familiar voice called, "Daryl Anne?"

I said a silent "Thank you, God" and exited the booth, reaching the door to greet my paternal grandmother. Wilhelmina Blessing—known to one and all as Billie—was tall and reed thin, her black hair twisted into its usual chignon, her blue eyes bright with excitement. She wore her favorite Chanel pantsuit, the right sleeve pushed up to accommodate the removable cast on her wrist.

She gave a few friendly waves, greeted her Bunko buddies, then steered me toward the counter. "Come on, I could use a cuppa."

"Me too," I said, glad for the company, even if adding caffeine to my already anxious nerves might not be such a great idea. I settled onto a stool beside her. "How's the wrist this morning?"

"A little weak." Billie did all the alterations for Blessing's Bridal, and she'd taught me how to sew when I was old enough to hold a needle and thread it. Six weeks ago, she'd slipped and broken her wrist, bringing me home from Los Angeles earlier than planned to help out in the bridal shop. Although the doctor pronounced her all healed last week, she claimed she wasn't taking chances. Thus the removable cast.

I suspected, however, it was a ploy to keep me home longer. Sadly, I was returning to L.A. the day after the wedding. I kissed her cheek, knowing how much I would miss doing that once I was back in California.

We ordered coffee, the old-fashioned kind, then she said, "You forgot to turn on your phone. I kept getting voice mail."

"I'm sorry." I'd turned off my phone when Meg was having

her meltdown. I pulled it from my pocket, turned it on, noting a couple of missed calls from Gram, but nothing else that required my immediate attention. I stirred cream into my coffee. "What's up? Is everything okay?"

"Fine. Better than fine." She stirred artificial sweetener into her coffee. "Exciting even. You know that reporter who's coming to interview everyone in town for that series of articles?"

"Yes." This advertising opportunity was more than a few articles. It was an Internet broadcast associated with a national network. I'd viewed a couple of sample shows, and it looked like a good deal that might benefit Blessing's Bridal as well as several other businesses in town.

"Well, we just got an e-mail from TR Jones," Billie said, setting her spoon on the saucer and ordering us each a warm, gooey cinnamon roll without asking if I wanted something else. I guessed the blueberry pancakes could wait for another day, but I raised an eyebrow at her selection.

She had Type 2 diabetes and Mom watched like a hawk over every bite of sugar that went into her mouth. Billie hated being told she couldn't do something and, even though it often led to disaster, like a broken wrist, she ignored what others thought was good for her and did whatever she damn-well pleased. Usually I admired that about her.

But not when it came to her health. She ignored my raised brow, forked a bite of cinnamon roll, and sighed with pleasure. "He wants to do our interview today. Now, before you protest, I didn't forget about Meg's final fitting or your girls' plans. So I figured early was better than later, get it over and done with, then you'll have the rest of the day free."

She sounded as though she was doing me a favor, and her

look said, "I've already set this up so please say *yes*." She lifted her cup and peered over its rim. "Okay?"

I thought about saying: *Sure. Why not? Why should anything go according to my plans today?* But I was not a martyr, and there was Meg to consider. She and Zelda still had their heads together discussing some last-minute details of the wedding or reception. And then she would talk to Big Finn. The cinnamon roll began to congeal in my stomach. Maid of honor duties aside, I couldn't just desert my best friend in her hour of need.

"What time did you tell him?"

She glanced at the clock over the door. "Nine o'clock."

It was 8:30. Barely enough time for us to get back to Blessings Bridal and for me to change clothes to something more suitable for an interview.

Billie gobbled down the last of her cinnamon roll as I pushed mine aside half eaten.

I said, "I'll have to tell Meg."

Billie's cell phone rang. "Your mother," she said. She answered, and the color drained from her face. "What? Are you sure?"

She handed me the phone. "She wants to speak to you."

"Mom, is something wrong?"

"Depends on your definition of right."

"What does that mean?"

"The people from the Internet are here with their cameras and lights and—"

"Oh, no. Tell them I'll be right there."

"It's not *them* you need to concern yourself with. It's *her*."

"Her?"

"The woman writing the articles."

I swear I heard venom in Mom's voice.

I frowned. "I thought the reporter was a man, a TR Jones."

"That's what she's calling herself these days, but she's still Tanya Reilly."

My mouth dropped open, and just as a hush fell over the café, I blurted out, "Meg's mother?"

From the end of the counter, I saw Big Finn's head snap in my direction.

Chapter 2

"Would you look at that fancy car?" Billie said as we neared Blessing's. Three blocks down from Cold Feet Café, the bridal shop has the town's largest parking lot, with Front Street on one side and Puget Sound at the far edge. Morning sun brush-stroked the solid brick building like an artist's watercolor painting. Once two lumber warehouses, the shop was now three stories of living and business space.

A brand-new, low-slung Jaguar with California plates was parked near the front entrance, and the sight of it both excited me and filled me with dread. "Crap."

Billie eyed me curiously.

"It's Peter Wolfe's car."

She stopped walking and gaped at me. "Peter Wolfe, the actor?"

"Peter is Meg's fiancé."

"Well, I'll be. I knew she was engaged to some actor, but I had no idea he was the star of the sitcom you both work on."

"Promise you won't tell your Bunko buddies until after the wedding. We are trying to keep this as low-key as possible."

She looked crestfallen. "Won't they be surprised, though."

As surprised as I was to see his car here. "He's not supposed to arrive until tomorrow," I muttered. My already skipping pulse kicked into overdrive. Was he inside with Meg's mom? I might actually throw up.

Billie huffed as if out of breath. "I specifically told everyone that the groomsmen fittings are tomorrow, not today."

"Peter isn't getting a tuxedo from us," I explained. "He has his own. He attends so many red carpet events in L.A., it's more practical to own than rent."

Billie frowned. "Then what *is* he doing here?"

Good question. And if he and Meg's mother had been introduced, if he realized who Tanya was, then all hell was breaking loose in the bridal shop.

"Well, he can't be here today, and that's all there is to it." Billie stomped her foot, indignation twisting her mouth. My grandmother was very old-fashioned and traditional, especially when it came to wedding superstitions. "Meg's final fitting is in an hour. W-What if he sees her gown? That's nothing but bad luck."

I'd happily be tasked with deterring bad luck superstitions rather than the looming calamity facing us. If it wasn't already too late. "Look, you keep Meg's mother busy while I get rid of Peter, okay?"

She looked as taken aback as if I'd poked her with a pin. "Me?"

"Yes, you." The idea seemed to sour her mood even more, but I didn't have time to wonder why. Not then.

We entered the private side door. The business office and elevator to the living quarters Billie and Mom shared on the third level were here as well as the stockroom. Mom was not in the office, and when we started toward the stockroom, she rushed at us like an enraged wasp, face red, eyes glazed and murderous.

I recoiled, not recognizing her at first. Susan Blessing was my rock, the queen of calm. She could take down a Bridezilla with a single raised eyebrow. She huffed, "I can't deal with that bi—"

She broke off. I don't think I'd ever heard her swear. Or seen her this close to it. She shoved past us and out the exit door, leaving us gaping after her. I started to ask what the deal was between my mom and Meg's, but Billie cut me off. "I'll go after Susan. You handle that wretched woman and Meg's fiancé. And make sure that groom doesn't see his bride's wedding gown."

Me? Handle them both? Oh, God. I nodded, reluctantly. I'd rather find my mother and learn the cause of her distress. I'd rather run off the end of the dock and into Puget Sound. I'd rather *anything* except what awaited in the salon. But I had to think of Meg. I wanted her wedding to be perfect. Or as perfect as possible under the circumstances.

Not to mention, the paramount duty of a maid of honor is to keep the bride emotionally calm. Who was going to keep me calm?

I bucked up, reminding myself that Peter had never met Tanya, and that Meg looked more like Big Finn than her mother. With my heart pounding and stomach pinching, I hurried through the stockroom full of racks of plastic-covered wedding gowns, past the dressing rooms and toward reception.

The main salon reminded me of a charming New York brownstone, the walls plaster-boarded with patches of aged brick showing through. Original hardwood planking and high ceilings made the space seem larger than it was. Fresh roses scented the air. Mannequins in the newest bridal attire decorated the three huge display windows with others placed prominently throughout the showroom floor. On the right side, two red velvet love-seats served as the waiting area. I ignored the couple sitting there, my gaze flying to the other end of the room, over the display rack of brochures from the various businesses in town and beyond the Edwardian reception desk.

Nothing overturned. No blazing guns smoking the air. No loud voices. Despite this good omen, my nerves were wound tighter than corset laces. Peter hated Meg's mother more than I did—if that were possible—for walking out on Meg when she was a kid. But since the reception area displayed no signs of an apocalypse, I could only assume the two had yet to introduce themselves. Could I be that lucky? Given Peter's penchant for privacy, maybe…

Or…another unnerving thought occurred to me. Had Meg failed not only to tell her father she'd invited Tanya to the wedding, but Peter as well?

Of course she had. Oh, God, Meg, what were you thinking? This was a ticking emotional bomb that no amount of organization or smoothing of ruffled feathers could defuse. Only she wasn't here to witness the fallout of her folly, to buffer the impact or spare innocent bystanders. Like me. The knot in my stomach grew melon-sized.

But I'd worried for nothing. Peter was not in the reception area. Only Tanya Reilly Jones and her camera tech—a rangy, long-haired guy with a mustache and different colored eyes. One blue, one hazel. A compact shoulder camcorder at his feet. They sat on the loveseat, conferring with their heads together. I heard my mother's name mentioned, and my dander flared. Whatever this woman had done to upset my usually easygoing mom was another checkmark against her. I'd never felt less like having a conversation with anyone.

As I struggled for composure, fifteen-year-old images tracked through my mind like a yellowed newsreel, recalling Tanya as a curvaceous brunette with bright brown eyes, a pretty face, and a loud laugh that squeezed like a vice. I knew, when she looked directly at me, I would see changes—age lines, weight gain, gray hairs? Warts, if karma prevailed.

Okay, scratch weight gain. She was thin, Hollywood-starlet thin, that kind of bobble-head thin. I supposed Internet video also put ten pounds on a person, but I hoped the loss of her voluptuous figure was due to guilt.

I interrupted their conversation. "I was expecting the usual interviewer from your show."

"I'm the producer of the show," Tanya said, staring at something on her phone, "but since this is my old stomping ground, I decided to handle the Weddingville interviews myself while I'm here for the wedding."

The guy beside her said, "Two birds with one stone."

Tanya lifted her head then, her eyes widening at the sight of me. Or maybe I just thought they'd widened. Now that I could see her face full on, I realized she had none of the age-defining wrinkles I'd expected. In fact, her skin was so tight that I doubted it could express any serious emotion. And when she stood, I corrected my original assessment. She hadn't lost any curves, although I suspected some curves were not natural. "My God, Daryl Anne Blessing. Why, you look so much like your father, Daryl, it just takes my breath."

Though this wasn't the first time I'd heard that, it was the first time the comparison to my late father sent a shiver down my spine. *Why? And why did Meg's mother remember my father so vividly after fifteen years—when I could barely recall his face?* Did it have anything to do with why my mother was so upset?

"Daryl was such a darling man," Tanya said, and I realized what had bothered me was the way she'd said Dad's name. As soft as a caress. I narrowed my eyes, giving her the opportunity to expand on that, but she began glancing away, twisting a ring on her pinkie finger. She changed the subject. "I appreciate your moving this interview up to this morning, especially since I know you weren't expecting us until tomorrow."

I bit my tongue to keep from saying, "We weren't expecting *you* at all." I also took a deep breath. I wanted to tell this woman what she could do with herself, wanted it so much I had to dig my fingernails into my palms to stop myself. I'd seen what bad press could do to lives, to businesses. Besides Meg, I had to consider how my actions might affect Mom and Billie, and this shop. I took a deep breath, gesturing to my outfit. "As you can see, I'm hardly interview-ready."

Tanya tilted her head, raking a gaze over me. "You look fine. And besides, I think your mother would prefer we do this and leave as quickly as possible."

The look on my sweet mother's face flashed through my mind, and my normally slow temper flashed like lightning. Indignation for Mom, and for Meg, took over my better judgment, and I blurted out, "You should probably expect a similar or somewhat worse reaction when others discover you're in town."

My bluntness brought Tanya standing a little straighter in her spiked heels. "Sticks and stones…"

I could tell the bravado was just that, and the unexpected vulnerability it exposed killed my mean-girl comeback. I'd spent so many years angry with this woman that I'd never even considered that she might have a different version of the past than the one I'd always heard. I shoved my hand through my hair and caught the lanky camera guy leaning in closer, hanging on our every word. I'd met a few of his type, one step above a paparazzo, always keying in on anything that he might sell to a gossip outlet. At the moment, he wasn't my problem. I didn't care what he thought.

Or what Tanya thought, I realized, surprising myself. "If you hurt Meg again," I said in a voice that chilled even me, "I will come after you."

Camera-guy glanced at his boss, waiting for her response. Tanya studied me for a few seconds, then said, "I'm glad Meg has a friend like you." She exhaled loudly. "Come on, Kramer, hike that camera to your shoulder, and let's get this interview started."

I caught my image in the camera lens and startled. I was not going to be coerced into an interview—that would be on the World Wide Web—wearing jeans and a sweatshirt, my short hair standing up in all the wrong places.

Tanya was grinning at me with something akin to delight, enjoying my discomfort. In that moment, I wanted to strangle her. But that would mean jail and a mug shot, and this ugly image on my record. Forever. Not to mention, it would ruin Meg's wedding. I closed my eyes and reeled in the anger as I might a cloth measuring tape, coiling it into a neat little ball until it was soft and pliable. Controllable.

For Meg's sake, I would be civil to this woman, even if it killed me.

And it just might.

"Turn off the camera, Kramer," I said, using the voice I reserved for actors who thought they could rifle through the rack of cast clothing I'd assigned and grab whatever outfit caught their eye, instead of what I'd chosen for their upcoming scenes. He ignored me like any good paparazzi would. I directed a glare at Tanya.

"Ms. Jones, exactly what is your intent for this Internet piece? Are you doing a documentary or a docudrama?"

"What?" The innocence in her wide eyes was as fake as her hair extensions.

I raised my voice and stared directly at the camera. "If you're really here to mend fences with your daughter, Ms. Jones, casting her maid of honor in a bad light on the Internet isn't going to work in your favor."

Tanya blanched. "Kramer, cut."

The green light on the camera blinked off, and Kramer relaxed like a starch-free petticoat.

"And delete the footage," I told him, glad to see him comply. I directed my next words to Tanya, using as sugary a tone as I could manage. "I have so many wedding details to see to today. I would really appreciate if we could do this interview tomorrow, as we'd originally scheduled, at ten a.m."

Tanya clearly didn't like someone else taking charge, but she nodded. "Ten sharp."

"Good. Meanwhile, I'm sure Meg will be glad to know you're in town." Even if Big Finn wouldn't be. "Why don't I give her a call and let her know?"

I reached into my pocket for my cell, but Tanya stopped me. "She knows."

Sure she does. And soon everyone else will too. I didn't need any more potential disasters rearing their ugly heads. *Like the blow-up that is bound to happen at the rehearsal dinner tomorrow night when Peter meets the mother who abandoned his bride-to-be. Like the aftershocks when Big Red comes face to face with his ex. Not to mention whatever secret resentment my mom holds against this woman.*

Like Scarlett, I decided to think about that tomorrow. Right now, I needed these two gone. I stepped back, gesturing toward the door. *The opening door.*

Peter Wolfe walked into the shop. Always fearing recognition and the ensuing fan adoration that usually accompanied it, he'd hidden his famous face behind huge sunglasses and a low-slung fedora. As if that would fool the two media idiots already standing in the reception area. My throat closed.

I rushed to him, blocking his view of Tanya and Kramer as best I could, given that he towered over me by six or more inches. I spoke in a low voice. "What are you doing here? We weren't expecting you until tomorrow."

"Ah, Daryl Anne," he said, giving me a boyish grin that was too practiced for my tastes. "From what little I've seen of this town, it's everything you and my fiancée claimed."

By which he meant: perfect for their secret wedding. Not that their getting married was secret, just the where and the when.

"Where is my fiancée, by the way?" he asked, speaking too loudly, his resonate voice carrying like a familiar song throughout the salon. "She's not answering her cell."

I felt Tanya and Kramer's gazes like hot pokers in my back. My pulse roared in my ears. I was pretty sure that by now, Meg was breaking the news to Big Finn about the newest addition to the guest list and not worrying about missed texts or phone calls. I couldn't figure out how to say that without eliciting World War III.

From the corner of my eye, I caught movement, the camcorder going to Kramer's shoulder, and knew his star-hunter nose had sniffed out the celebrity hidden in a flimsy disguise. I spun to see the *record* light glowing green. Kramer said, "Hey, Peter, what are you doing in Weddingville?"

My heart literally stopped beating.

"What the hell?" Peter said, his mouth twisting as he jerked toward Kramer. His fists balled. I realized he was about to pull an Alex Baldwin or Kanye West on the photographer. "Shit. I knew it was too good to be true. You promised there wouldn't be any paparazzi in this little village, Daryl Anne. Otherwise I wouldn't have agreed to hold the wedding here."

Before I could assimilate that Peter had just told the press about the secret wedding, or assure Peter that Kramer was not paparazzi, Tanya stepped forward. "Hello, Peter."

"What the fuck?" Kramer growled, whirling on Tanya. "This is the guy who's marrying your daughter?"

"*Your* daughter?" Peter went pale beneath his tan, looking as if he might be sick.

Tanya was nodding, stepping toward Peter with a grin. "Surprise."

Oh. God. I groaned silently. The opening lines of a favorite historical novel flashed through my mind. Although the author and title eluded me just then, the gist of the scene did not. *It was only a matter of minutes before the wedding party began killing each other.* And this wasn't even the rehearsal dinner.

Chapter 3

Kramer looked as upset as Peter, but I'd seen the actor's temper flare, seen heads roll with one flick of his razor-sharp tongue, and while I expected he'd lash into Tanya, instead he snarled at me. "Where's Meg?"

"Cold Feet Café," I said, pointing down the street. "Peter, I—" He wasn't listening. He stormed out. A second later, the Jaguar roared to life, leaving the parking lot on squealing tires, heading up the street away from Big Finn's diner. I had no time to wonder where he was going.

"What an asscap!" Tanya's cheeks bloomed a brilliant pink.

But Kramer's complexion was blood red as he glared at her. "Why didn't you tell me your daughter is marrying Peter Wolfe?"

Tanya shook her head, blowing him off, but Kramer wasn't having any of it. He grabbed her arm and made her look at him. "Why?"

"Why do you think?" Tanya muttered, obviously not liking that I was being given a peek behind the façade of their seemingly stellar working relationship. Her jaw clenched. "Let go of me. Now."

Kramer held on for several more beats, then threw his fingers wide, as though really letting go. I had a vision of Tanya falling to the hard plank floor, her head thunking like a ripe melon. It didn't happen, but I could dream, couldn't I?

"I take it Meg hasn't told Peter about inviting me to the wedding," Tanya said, looking as though that were my fault.

"That would be my guess as well," I said.

"Like mother, like daughter," Kramer muttered.

* * *

By the time, Meg arrived for her final dress fitting, I had a stress headache starting in my temples and spreading across my skull, making me long for some Extra Strength Tylenol. I had found time to shower and change, but all of my questions to my mother about Tanya Reilly Jones had fallen on deaf ears.

Billie was equally zip-lipped on the subject, and it was like the elephant in the room, bigger and whiter than Meg's Cinderella-style gown. As I gazed at my best friend, I felt something like awe catch inside my chest. She was stunning. The champagne tone gave her pale, lightly freckled skin a peaches and cream hue, but the red around her eyes told me things hadn't gone well with Big Finn. The need to cheer her up washed through me. "You're absolutely gorgeous, Meg."

"Prettiest bride we've had in a while," Mom agreed, but her smile didn't reach her eyes, which I hoped Meg wouldn't notice. I could tell my friend was hanging on to her composure by a thread, at best. We had not had a moment alone to discuss anything before Mom and Billie joined us, and given my mother also sported red-rimmed eyes, I had curbed my need-to-know on all fronts.

For now.

But the moment we headed out for our girls' day, I expected details, at least from my bestie. Mom and Billie would be harder nuts to crack.

"I always thought you'd be marrying Troy in a dress like this," Billie said, dropping a bomb in the room.

Meg's flinched as if my grandmother had just pinched her. Troy O'Malley was a hometown boy, the only guy Meg ever dated before moving to L.A. A strange little laugh escaped my best friend as she avoided my gaze in the mirror.

"What do you think, Meg?" my mother asked, moving the subject back to the dress and off of old boyfriends and broken hearts.

Meg glanced at herself in the mirror. A tiny gasp slipped from her, and tears welled in her eyes. I braced for a deluge. But only a single droplet dampened her cheek, pushed out by a swell of emotion. She was a bride seeing herself in a wedding gown that looked and felt as if it were created for her alone. Meg waved her hands near her cheeks, fanning away other impending tears, smiling. "Oh, Susan, Billie, I didn't know I could feel so…so… pretty. Thank you so very much."

"Well, Daryl Anne's the one who saved the day." Billie held up her wrist, indicating that I'd done most of the alterations needed on the gown. "You can thank her, dear."

"Oh, I do. Every day." Meg squeezed my hand, and I swallowed over a knot of loving emotion that had lodged in my throat.

I led her back to the dressing room and helped her out of the gown, putting it into a protective covering where it would stay until the final pressing before the wedding. But I couldn't contain my curiosity a moment longer. "So what happened with your dad?"

Meg rolled her eyes as she wiggled into her jeans. "He was pissed. That-vein-at-his-temple-might-burst furious."

This didn't surprise me. "Did he scream at you in front of all the customers?" In other words, the whole town?

"I took him into his office to tell him. I gave Zelda a heads-up first though, and she burst in when she heard him swear. I don't know what it is about that woman, but Dad listened to her. She said just the right things, and he calmed down. He's not happy about seeing Mom, but he said he won't make a scene."

"As long as she doesn't?"

Meg nodded. "Yeah, something like that."

I tried not to imagine the disaster I felt brewing on the horizon like storm clouds whirling into a tornado.

"He says he won't come to the rehearsal dinner if she's there, but I don't know how to tell her."

Not telling people things seems to be a very big problem for you lately, my darling BFF. I refrained from saying it. I cleared my throat. "Uh, sweetie, Big Finn isn't the only guy unhappy about your mother coming to the wedding."

Meg frowned, fixing her hair in the mirror. "What do you mean?"

"Peter was here today."

"In town?" Her eyes widened as she caught my gaze.

"In the bridal shop. When Tanya was here." I gave that a moment to sink in, then said, "And of course, she and her cameraman recognized him right off."

Meg seemed to be holding her breath.

Since I didn't want her turning blue, I rushed on. "At first Peter thought they were paparazzi, but then the camera guy asked Tanya if Peter was the actor marrying her daughter."

"Holy shit." Meg groaned, covering her eyes, mumbling something I couldn't discern. When she lowered her hand, I read dread in her eyes. "What did Peter do?"

There was no guilt or contrition on her part, just curiosity. She wasn't taking any responsibility for this fiasco. I recalled Kramer words: like mother, like daughter. I resisted the urge to shake her. "Strangely, your fiancé got in his car and left. Hasn't he texted or phoned you?"

"I had a text from him, but I didn't see it until I was done speaking to Dad. All Peter said was that he was staying in Seattle at some fancy hotel where he could have privacy, and that he'd see me at the rehearsal dinner tomorrow night." Meg looked up from tying her sneakers.

Well, at least he wasn't calling off the wedding. I supposed that was something to be thankful for, even if this odd behavior was completely unlike the quick-tempered man I knew on the set of our sitcom.

Meg gave herself one last glance in the mirror, probably wishing for something to clear the redness from her eyes. She said, "I didn't know Peter was driving up from Los Angeles. I thought he was flying in tomorrow and renting a car at the airport."

"Obviously, he changed his mind." My headache stabbed like needles, and I realized the only thing that would help was food. "Let's go get some lunch. All this drama has given me such an appetite."

In fact, I'd be lucky to eat much at all, even though my head was begging me to.

Meg made a face. "Please don't be mad. I need to cancel our girls' day. I'm meeting Mom for lunch. She wanted to have some time together to catch up before the rehearsal dinner and wedding. And you and I will be together tonight at the bachelorette party."

Disappointment stabbed through me. I'd really been looking forward to some alone time with Meg and instead found myself chocking up another resentment against Tanya Reilly Jones. But I just nodded. I couldn't put myself in Meg's shoes. My mother hadn't run out on me. I didn't ever feel that ache for a mom that Meg must have felt, even as she denied it. If she needed to do this, I needed to support her in it.

And yet, something had been swirling around in my curiosity zone. "How did you find Tanya? I mean, I didn't even know you were looking for her."

"Oh, she found me." Meg gazed up at me with a smile in her green eyes. "She said she saw an article in the *Hollywood Review*. You know, the one about 'TV heart throb gets engaged to unknown makeup artist, Meg Reilly.' Remember that one?"

I did. "Considering she left when you were eleven, I find it quite a leap for her to assume the Meg Reilly engaged to Peter Wolfe would be you."

"She said she's subscribed to *The Weddingville Weekly* for years and read that I'd moved to L.A. to follow my dream of becoming a makeup artist. Not such a leap. But she researched like a little bloodhound until she knew for certain."

More like a ferret. As I walked Meg to the door, I wondered if Tanya was really here for Meg, or to establish herself as Peter Wolfe's mother-in-law and garner all the personal benefit she thought would come with that honor. Money. Social status. Power. I kept the thought to myself.

At the door, Meg turned, grinning. "I wasn't going to tell you until we were at lunch, but guess who I ran into as I was leaving Cold Feet Café?"

Seriously, did she expect me to name the whole town? It could be anyone. "Um. I give up. Who?"

"Troy."

My mouth fell open.

"I almost fainted when Billie said that about my marrying Troy. As if she knew I'd seen him right before I came here for my appointment."

Meg had been in love, off and on, with Troy O'Malley since they were both five years old. They'd gone together most of their junior and high school years. The whole town had always assumed that they'd marry one day. Their sudden breakup had shocked everyone. Last I'd heard Troy was deployed overseas somewhere with the navy. "He's back in town? On leave?"

"Nope. Remember how he planned on being a career naval officer?"

How could I forget? It was what had caused their final split.

"Well, he decided not to reenlist after his four-year stint." Conflict floated across her eyes like a stream of swift-moving clouds. Meg nibbled her lower lip. "How come you didn't you know he was back in town and working with the local police department?"

"Because no one told me," I said, wondering how I'd managed to not hear this bit of gossip. "And since I've been home, I haven't run into him."

"Well, when you do, you're in for a treat. He's sexy as hell in his uniform."

"Says the woman who is two days away from getting married."

"I know, I know. But I'm not dead. I can still look and appreciate."

And remember. The twinkling in her emerald eyes suggested more than female admiration for a well-built, handsome male. Maybe yearning? Or desire? No, please, no. Disquiet scurried through my tummy like stampeding mice. Why had I suggested Peter and Meg tie the knot in Weddingville?

I asked, "You're not having second thoughts about marrying Peter, are you?"

"God no." Meg balked. "That would be insane…right?"

"Yes." Insane. Nuts. Chaotic. Just like Meg. I groaned silently. Forget lunch; I was heading straight to the wine bottle in the fridge.

Meg gathered her purse and squeezed my hand. "I've got to run. Mom's waiting for me. Oh, wow, saying that out loud just gave me chills."

Yeah, me too. I glanced back and saw something on the dressing room counter. "Hey, don't forget this."

Meg snatched her phone from me and sighed. "Sometimes I wish I could."

I nodded. Unlike most of our peers, she hadn't owned a cell phone until just before moving to Los Angeles. Big Finn said he wouldn't have his daughter wasting her time staring at some small screen when all the news that was relevant could be learned at his café over breakfast, lunch, or dinner. She was forever setting the phone down, forgetting where she'd put it, and walking off without it.

"Don't forget, we have to be at Violet's at eight pm," I reminded her. "The limo is picking us up there."

"Oh, I'll be there. Tonight we celebrate!"

* * *

It's funny how you can make arrangements, double check to be sure everyone is following through on their end, and then, being anal about details, triple check, and still have it not turn out as expected. What did the universe have against me? The limo was late to Violet's to pick us up and take us to the Emerald Queen Casino for the bachelorette party. Champagne flowing. Check. Giggling, rowdy women. Check. Loud music and dancing. Check.

Ex-boyfriend of bride-to-be? Not supposed to be there. Chills went through me—not the excited kind either, but the bad, bad feeling kind. What was Troy O'Malley doing at the casino with a group of his buddies? Who told him where we'd be?

And why had he dragged Tanya Reilly Jones along?

"A penny for your thoughts," a man's voice said near my ear. I inhaled the sandalwood scent, so much like my father's had been that I actually flushed, half-expecting to find Daddy there when I turned around.

I eased slowly in the man's direction, noting a head of tawny, windblown hair, and found myself gazing up into the warmest brown eyes I'd ever seen. Seth Quinlan, the owner of Weddingville's Cherished Moments photo studio, hovered near my shoulder. My heart did a happy little skip at the sight of him. He gave me his crooked smile, the one that melted my insides, the one that wouldn't work on a more handsome visage but that on Seth's rugged face was just the right asset to turn almost homely into stunningly sexy.

He'd always thought of me as one of the guys, however, totally ignorant of my secret crush on him. And no wonder. If anything, he was more attractive than ever in faded jeans that hugged his lean hips and a Tommy Bahama shirt that showcased broad shoulders and muscled arms. *Whew. Sexy romantic lead.* I couldn't have dressed him better.

"What are you doing here?" I asked, meaning what are Troy and his gang doing here?

"I came with Troy. He said something about Meg's mom inviting him."

Meg's mom had invited him? Really? And who'd invited her? I eyed Tanya, taking in her head-turning, skintight leopard-print dress and hot-pink five-inch heels. If this were a Hollywood set, I'd tag that outfit for Courtney Cox's character on *Cougar Town*. "This is supposed to be a bachelorette party. No men allowed."

"Unless you're stripping." Katie Lancaster, bridesmaid number one, was a ditzy brunette, with wide gray eyes and a grating voice. She squealed, grabbing the edge of Seth's shirt, and tugging it upward, aided by Jade Warren, bridesmaid number two. The wide blue streak in her long dark hair bounced as she gave me the evil eye. We were tolerating each other for Meg's sake.

Violet Pringle, bridesmaid number three, blushed and giggled, then clamped her hand over her mouth and looked away as though she might burn in hell if she were caught staring at a man's naked six-pack.

I glanced up at Ash Moon, all five-foot-ten inches of her. She was Meg's assistant, and she seemed neither shocked nor titillated by the shenanigans of the bridesmaids. Growing up in Los Angeles, she'd probably seen it all. Too many times. Her doe eyes were heavily made up, her flyaway hair shoulder-length, her lean curves willowy in a vintage Chanel dress that she'd confided cost only pennies. *Note to self: go shopping with Ash when you return to L.A.* Ash gestured toward Troy, and whisper-asked, "Who's the hunk flirting with Meg?"

"Ex-boyfriend." I kept my tone even, struggling not to judge Troy's motives.

Ash frowned. "I guess he didn't get the memo."

"What memo?"

"That Meg is getting married in a couple of days. I should set him straight."

I caught her arm, intent on avoiding a scene. Ash tended to be protective of Meg. Not a bad trait in an assistant, but not good in this situation. "Let's let Meg handle it, okay?"

She glanced at Meg, then nodded. "Okay. But who's the cougar who came with him? His mom?"

"Meg's mom."

Ash gasped. "But…I thought Meg hated her?"

I sighed. "It seems they've recently reconciled."

An emotion flashed through Ash's pale green eyes. Betrayal? Envy? I couldn't be sure. "Wow."

Yeah, wow. My attention returned to Seth and the overly zealous bridesmaids tugging on his shirt. He laughed, while I bit down the insane urge to slap Katie and Jade. Especially Jade. As if I had some kind of claim on the man. *In my dreams.*

Seth did his own untangling, backing out of the reach of grabby hands, but Troy had no such inhibition. "If that's what it takes," he said, as he boogied up to Meg, his T-shirt halfway up his stomach, exposing a six-pack that would make Coors drool.

Meg seemed to feel that way about it too. She blushed and stared, her fingers waggling upward, gesturing for Troy to go all the way. He'd filled out during his stint in the navy, I noticed, broader shoulders, big guns, and his chin a bit stronger. There was something worldly in his eyes that was very sexy, and he'd traded in the sloppy, unkempt hair of his youth for a short, trim cut that enhanced his steely, black-haired, blue-eyed appeal. It wasn't lost on Meg either.

I gave myself a shake. This was a disaster. I had to break the spell these two seemed caught up in. "You want security to toss us out?"

I was being elbowed aside; the hem of Troy's shirt rose higher.

"Troy, you're breaking the law."

He froze, his eyes widened, and he glanced around, nodding reluctantly. He tugged his shirt down over his bare skin, but before I could shoo him away, he grabbed Meg and pulled her onto the dance floor, just as a slow song began playing. A favorite song of theirs. Had Troy asked the band to play this tune? Or was karma messing with me?

"Aren't they the cutest couple," Tanya said, a dreamy smile on her face.

I couldn't deny it. The chemistry they'd shared as teenagers flared anew, sizzling the air around them. If they were testing for the role of lovers in a film, they'd be hired on the spot. My stomach did a sickening flip. "Meg is marrying Peter."

"She could do better."

Better than a famous actor making half a million a week? I would bet Tanya would snap up a marriage proposal from someone like Peter. I blinked. Were Meg and Troy snuggling? Oh my God, they were. And Tanya had her cell phone out, snapping photos of their shenanigans.

"What are you doing?"

"I've been taking photos all day." She kept the phone trained on Troy and Meg dancing, grinning at each other. "I want to put together an album for Meg, and I admit it, for myself."

Of Meg with her ex-boyfriend's hand on her ass? I made a

grab for Tanya's phone, intending to delete all the images, but she anticipated me. "Oh no, you don't."

She shoved the phone into her bra and scowled at me. "You're a real party poop, you know that?"

"And you're a real bitch!" I shouted as the music stopped. And now shocked faces were gaping at me. But the most shocking thing was Meg's reaction.

Chapter 4

Two days before the wedding

As I shuffled into the kitchen, tugging my bathrobe around me, Billie handed me a cup of coffee, hot and steaming, as black as my mood.

"You look like something the dog dragged in, chewed up, pissed on, and tossed back out, Daryl Anne," she said.

Yep, that was exactly how I felt, but all I said was, "Hmm."

"Must have been some bachelorette party," Mom said, opening the blinds on the third-floor loft apartment where she and Billie and I had moved after losing Dad. On this side of the building, the combined living room and kitchen windows overlooked Puget Sound, while the three bedroom windows all faced Front Street. "We didn't have bachelorette parties when I married your father. Just a bridal shower with silly gifts."

"And sillier games," Billie added, huffing. "Nowadays they get drunk and have strippers. You did have a stripper, didn't you?"

"No," I said, trying not to recall the flash of enticing male abs both Troy and Seth had momentarily exposed. *I really need to get a boyfriend.*

"I bet it was a lot of fun," Mom said.

Fun was not how I'd describe what occurred the previous evening. I went in search of some Extra Strength Tylenol to go with my coffee and hangover. Actually, I wasn't hung over. I'd had a total of one and a half glasses of champagne before Seth drove me home. He'd insisted on stopping for something to eat, and we'd shared a carafe of coffee, which probably contributed to my sleeplessness. Living in Hollywood, I saw too many coworkers and friends throw their careers—and often their lives—away to the lure of alcohol and drugs, prescription or street. So far, my vices included only the occasional glass or two of wine.

"Don't you have a lot of things to do before the rehearsal dinner tonight?" Billie said.

"Hmm." I knew my responses might seem odd, but what else could I say? After last night, I wasn't sure about anything on today's schedule. Did Tanya Reilly Jones and Kramer intend to keep their appointment this morning? Was Big Finn coming to the rehearsal dinner? Would Meg and I make up? I couldn't discuss any of it just now as it was bound to stir up questions I hadn't even thought of yet. Besides, I was pretty sure I couldn't speak more than three consecutive words without my head cracking wide open.

"Well," Mom said, easing onto the kitchen barstool beside me while I swallowed the pain medicine, "Seth phoned. He wants to stop by in about an hour if you can spare him some time. Something about photos for the dinner tonight."

I groaned, and both Billie and Mom eyed me with concern. Billie said, "Hardly the reaction we expected."

Yes. They both knew about my teenage crush. But surely I didn't need to explain that I wasn't going to pursue a romance with a man in Weddingville when I would be heading back to Los Angeles next week? Or, for that matter, that he still didn't see me as more than one of the boys. Just a friend. A pal. The kind you took pity on when the limo that had brought you to the party left without you.

I felt my mother's warm hand land on my shoulder. "What's going on, Daryl Anne?"

I jerked, guilt darting through me. There was no hiding my feelings from this woman. She knew me too well. My incoherent mutterings had only proven to her that I was upset. I took a sip of coffee, set it down, and slowly met her gaze. "I called Meg's mom a bitch last night, right to her face, and Meg might not be speaking to me any longer."

Mom's eyes grew as round as cupcakes. "Tanya was invited to the bachelorette party?"

"Well, not exactly. She sort of crashed it…at the casino."

"Well, I hope you didn't call her that for Susan's sake," Billie said, as if I knew why I would need to verbally beat up Tanya for whatever she had done to my mother. I looked from one to the other, hoping for enlightenment, but none was offered.

"Why did you call her the B word?" Mom asked, feigning a mild interest despite leaning toward me with the teeniest glint in her eye.

I considered being as closed mouth to them as they'd been to me, but I knew they'd worm it out of me. "She was taking a bunch of photos of Meg and Troy dancing. She said she was going to make a photo album for Meg."

"Troy O'Malley was at the party too?" Mom's eyebrows twitched.

"Tanya came with him and some of his buddies," I said.

"I told you, Susan. An alley cat doesn't change its spots," Billie said, then turned confused eyes on me. "I thought Meg was marrying Peter the actor."

"She is, Gram. That's the point. Why would Tanya make an album with photos of Meg and Troy dancing?"

"Probably plans on giving it as a wedding present," Billie said.

"Wouldn't put it past her," Mom muttered, something akin to hellfire burning through her words. I had the sense that, if Tanya were standing in our kitchen right now, she'd be ashes. Mom sighed loudly, then went for more coffee.

"Gonna be a five-pot day," Billie grumbled.

But Mom gave herself a shake and offered me a tender smile like the one she'd given me whenever I came to her as a child with scraped knees. "You and Meg have been friends a long time, sweetheart. Sometimes friends have spats, especially good friends, but true friends can work through anything. You'll see. I'm sure she's not mad. Not really."

Well, I'm mad at her. She left me at the casino with no way to get home. I stopped short of saying it out loud. As much as I wanted them to be Team Daryl Anne, I also didn't want there to be Meg on one side and me on the other of any controversy. If she didn't call or text in the next hour, I'd hunt her down, and we'd duke it out. Verbally.

After all, the paramount duty of the maid of honor was to keep the bride-to-be emotionally calm. A sickening thought occurred to me. Was I still the maid of honor? Or had Meg decided she'd rather Tanya take over that prize role? No. She wouldn't do that to me…would she? I swallowed coffee, considering. If I knew Meg, and I did, she was in hyper-chaotic mode about now, unable to think straight with all the unplanned, unprepared-for drama and nostalgia coming at her.

Another awful thought hit me. What had gone on at the bachelorette party after they left the casino? Had Troy spent the whole evening with Meg? Perhaps the night? *Oh, God, no, not that.* I groaned again.

"Maybe you should go back to bed. You really don't look well, Daryl Anne," Mom said.

"Maybe somebody slipped her one of those roo-fees last night," Billie said. "Did you black out any time during the evening or later?"

I frowned at Billie, but that sent a sharp jab of pain straight to my temples. I shuffled off to my bedroom. No one had drugged me. I wasn't hung over. I was stressed. My plans and sense of calm were as shattered as a glass slipper. As I showered, dressed, applied lipstick and mascara, the same thought kept whirling through my head. Whatever Meg was thinking, whatever she was doing, I had to try to help her make it through.

* * *

I knocked on Meg's motel cabin, praying that wasn't Troy's pickup parked in front of the cabin next door. Had it only been yesterday that I'd been standing on this same stoop, my heart full of excitement for my best friend in all this world? How could I now—a mere twenty-four hours later—feel my knees knocking harder than my hand hitting the door? As if that weren't bad enough, my stomach churned, and my pulse skipped. Weirdly, some little part of me clung to the absurd notion that Meg hadn't really meant to leave me at the casino. That this was a bad dream brought on by my own pre-wedding jitters. Could the maid of honor have pre-wedding jitters?

Yeah, probably not. I hit the door again. *Come on Meg. Fling open the door. Be glad to see me so we can exchange apologies.* Yes, I should be furious that she'd abandoned me at the casino, but she'd been under the influence. Of champagne. Of her mother. Of her former lover.

Then why hasn't she texted or phoned?

And why wasn't she answering the door? I glanced at the pickup again, and the churning in my stomach turned to a sick sensation. I rapped harder. "Meg? It's me, Daryl Anne."

I stood there, listening for sounds on the other side of the door, shuffling feet, muffled voices, the shower running. Something. Nothing. Still, I knocked a couple of more times before giving up.

With an ache settling in my chest right beside the anger I'd banked, I started back toward Front Street, walking numbly past shop windows gaily displaying essential wedding accessories. Everywhere I looked seemed to mock me. The ousted maid of honor.

I didn't want to go back to the bridal shop, couldn't face Mom and Billie. Or Seth. I glanced around and realized I was standing outside Cold Feet Café. It appeared that the morning rush had come and gone, but there were still diners enjoying breakfast. I shoved inside, immediately inhaling the mouthwatering aromas of coffee, bacon, and toast. My stomach growled. Maybe the churning was partially hunger.

"Good morning, Daryl Anne," several of the folks I've known since childhood said in unison, and some of my anxiety dissolved like sugar in hot tea, easing my tummy ache. I had to admit that there was something wonderful about not being anonymous in a public eatery. I couldn't go anywhere alone in Los Angeles and feel this sense of belonging.

I slipped onto a stool at the counter, accepted a cup of coffee, and ordered an egg with toast and bacon. I glanced around. I didn't know what I was looking for, or who I might be hoping to find here, but I noticed a flash of color flapping in one of the booths. I blinked and focused. Zelda Love, Meg's wedding planner, was waving at me, signaling me to join her.

Ah, what the heck? Maybe she could tell me what was going on with Big Finn, at least. I told the waitress I was moving and carried my coffee to the booth.

"Just the person I was hoping to track down today," Zelda said as I sat opposite her. She brought to mind a brilliant parrot with her spiky yellow hair, and wild blue, red, and green billowing top. Her stuffed notebook sat to one side of a large mug of coffee.

"I was hoping to speak with you today too." But now that that opportunity was leaning eagerly toward me across the table, I wasn't sure just how to broach the subject of Meg and Big Finn's argument yesterday. It wasn't as if Zelda didn't know about it. But somehow, it seemed like none of my business, despite it being totally my business if I were still the maid of honor. That was the crux of it. Was I or wasn't I? Maybe I should just hand over what I did have planned to Zelda and let her and my ex-best friend work it out.

Zelda's phone beeped. "It's a text. I need to answer right away. Do you mind?"

"No. Take it." I checked my phone, hoping to also find a text. Nope. Nothing. Okay, I admit it. The longer I went without any response from Meg, the more pissed I was getting. Who could blame me? I'd been trying to justify Meg's actions, damning myself the worst kind of friend for calling out her mother, but by now she should have made some effort to contact me. This silent wall was too much.

The waitress delivered my breakfast. I waited until she'd left us alone before asking in a lowered voice, "What's the deal with Big Finn and the rehearsal dinner?"

Zelda rolled her eyes and sighed. "I've been trying to reason with him, but that big Irish temper isn't coming around very fast."

I nibbled on a piece of bacon, glancing at the wall clock, calculating. Less than eight hours before the wedding rehearsal and the dinner immediately after. "Do you know if he's going to be at the chapel, at least? He is still planning on giving Meg away, isn't he?"

I heard a little edge in my voice and took a sip of coffee, and then dug into my egg.

"I'm not sure about the dinner, but he won't let that woman keep him from walking his daughter down the aisle. He's telling Meg that right now." She crooked an elbow toward the back of the diner.

My gaze followed suit, my vision locking on the closed office door. Meg was with her dad? Not with Troy? I ought to be relieved; instead a knot filled my stomach, and I shoved my half-eaten food aside. "I'm glad. She would be devastated if he didn't."

"Well, there is a caveat. He won't do it if Meg even suggests that Tanya also walk her down the aisle."

"Meg wouldn't—" I broke off. Considering the things Meg had been doing the past twenty-four hours, I was no longer certain what she might or might not do. "Why did you want to speak to me, Zelda?"

"At the dinner tonight, if Finn does attend... I'll be with him... as his date."

And this was my business, why? Did she think I was in charge of who sat next to who at the dinner? I thought that was her job. "Er, are you two dating?"

"Five months now." A telltale blush of pink spread across her cheeks. My heart warmed at the thought of Big Finn finding romance after so many years alone and, although I never would have matched Zelda with him, it didn't seem so odd-couple now that I thought about it. He was like a grizzly on the surface, gruff, loud, opinionated, but with a teddy bear center. She was like a kitten who would go where danger lived and never suspect she should be afraid. If anyone could bring Big Finn's softer side to the surface more often, I suspected it might be Zelda.

I smiled. "I wonder why Meg didn't mention this..."

Zelda winced. "I'm not sure Finn has told her yet."

Why not? "Well, congratulations. He's a really great guy." I bit into another piece of bacon.

"He is, isn't he?" She pressed her lips together and leaned toward me. "I was wary at first, given my history with that ex of his, about even getting to know him."

I choked on the bacon. "History? You know Tanya?"

Her nose wrinkled as if I'd shoved her face into a pile of garbage. "We went to school together in Tacoma. Lincoln High. I'd lost touch with her when I married and moved to Anaheim. I wish I'd never heard from her again."

"What did she do to you?"

"Shortly after losing my husband, I opened a small wedding planning business. Tanya e-mailed me out of the blue. She said she was producing an online magazine and wondered if I'd be interested in doing an interview. I jumped at the opportunity to boost my visibility and to reconnect with my former classmate." She tugged on her hair as she spoke. "We met for lunch, caught up on each other's lives, and then settled in to the business at hand."

"I take it the article didn't go well?"

Pink scored Zelda's cheeks. "I thought we were doing an interview about the benefits of hiring a wedding planner, but the end result was a business killer. My words were taken out of context, cut and pasted into a humorous clip that made me look like an incompetent twit. I lost potential clients and the first celebrity wedding I'd snagged."

"Oh my God, that's awful."

"That's why I need your help, Daryl Anne. Keep that witch away from Finn and me, or I can't be held accountable for what I might do to her."

I think my mouth fell open. Was she suggesting violence? Sweet little Zelda? Apparently the kitten had tiger claws. Before I could respond, I spied two redheads at the far end of the diner.

Meg and her father. They weren't shouting, but Big Finn wasn't smiling either. He seemed to be telling his daughter something similar to what Zelda had just said. I stood as Meg walked toward me, head bent, gaze riveted to her cell phone, nibbling on her lower lip, a sure sign of stress. When she reached me, she glanced up and froze.

Chapter 5

Daryl Anne," Meg's face flashed guilt, her eyes a mix of dread and something I couldn't read. "I…"

"No." I caught her arm, aware of curious stares and a sudden lull in conversation. I lowered my voice until only she could hear and spoke through clenched teeth, "We're not having this conversation here."

But we weren't having the conversation at all, it seemed. The moment we were alone on the sidewalk, her phone announced a text message. Then another. And another. Meg's complexion was suddenly so pale even her freckles looked white.

Her voice shook when she said, "They're from Peter. Someone Instagrammed photos to him of Troy and me dancing last night." She swallowed hard, dread swimming in her eyes. "He wants to talk. He's picking me up—" The roar of the Jaguar coming up the street cut her off. Meg squawked, "Now."

The sleek car slid to the curb, its passenger door swinging wide. Peter barked, "Get in. Quick. Before those paparazzi scumbags catch sight of me."

"I'm sorry," Meg mumbled at me as she slipped into the car

and was gone as fast as a bug swallowed by a giant toad. She'd barely shut the door when Peter gunned the engine.

Exhaust fumes swirled into my nose, the foul stench leaving a bad taste in my mouth. I wanted to shout to Peter that he might want to heed the warnings and dangers of texting while driving, but they were rapidly disappearing up Front Street. I exhaled in frustration.

As I started toward the bridal shop, I began wondering why Meg had said she was sorry. Sorry about what? For leaving me at the casino? For dirty dancing with her ex-lover? Or that Peter had found out?

Peter. Found. Out. The realization slammed into me as though I'd heard a gunshot a few minutes earlier and was only now feeling the bullet's impact. Oh, God. This was exactly what I'd worried would happen last night when Troy crashed the bachelorette party. When Tanya began taking photos. *Tanya.*

This was her fault. It was all her fault. Meg leaving me at the casino. Meg dancing with Troy. *Did it make me a bad person that I wanted to do murderous things to her?* I groaned. I was going to hell. I caught my reflection in a shop window and was surprised not to see steam coming out of my ears. Rage burned through me, heating my cheeks. My hands curled into fists at my sides.

I zeroed in on Blessing's Bridal, quickening my step, hoping Tanya and Kramer were waiting to do our interview. No one messed with this maid of honor. But as I sucked in the salty sea air, it seemed to clear my head and cool my jets. Anger ebbed from me like the morning tide, a little more with every step, leaving a wide shoreline of doubt. Was I jumping to conclusions in thinking Tanya had Instagrammed the photo to Peter? The main thing in her favor: He hated her, which meant he hadn't given her his phone number.

I stopped, waiting for a group of early morning shoppers, a bride-to-be and her entourage, shoving into the bridal shop, giggling. Their excitement was palpable, but it didn't lift my spirits. My mind raced. If not Tanya, who might have sent Peter the photos? Anyone at the party or at the casino could have snapped shots of Troy and Meg dancing, but not anyone could have sent those pictures to Peter's phone. Not without having his cell number. That narrowed the suspect list to Meg. Me. And maybe—though I couldn't be sure—Meg's assistant. I didn't do it. I couldn't see Meg doing it. But Ash didn't seem likely either. She'd been covering everything at work, allowing Meg to concentrate on the wedding. Then who?

Disquiet spread through me. This mess was my fault. I hadn't stayed vigilant at the bachelorette party. I'd allowed myself to engage in the fun, forgetting that part of the maid of honor's duty in keeping the bride emotionally calm was to foresee the danger in partygoers with smart phones. It just hadn't occurred to me that I'd need to worry about one of our friends wanting to derail the wedding. But apparently someone did. And if the conversation Meg and Peter were having right now didn't go well, that someone was going to get their wish.

* * *

Tanya and Kramer didn't show up. Meg did. Her usually sparkly green eyes were dull, swollen, streaked red. My heart stopped, then filled with compassion and pity. Don't get me wrong, I was still pissed at being left at the casino, but we'd been friends too long for me to turn away when she was hurting this much. I couldn't be that cruel.

Obviously, the wedding was off.

The methodical side of my brain began chocking up the list of calls I'd be making soon. The caterer. The restaurant for the rehearsal dinner. The florist. The wedding site. The guests. I took her upstairs to our family quarters. I poured us each a cup of coffee, and we sat on cushions on the floor next to the coffee table as we'd done so often through our teens. The morning sun poured in the windows. I said, "I'm sorry about the wedding, but I was afraid this was going to happen when Troy showed up last night and, and—"

"And we got in a fight?" Meg said, putting it out there. Evidently, she wanted to clear the air as much as I did. "I won't apologize for being pissed. Everyone is hating on my mom, and it's ruining my wedding."

I recalled Zelda's warning. Apparently the meeting Meg had had with her dad ended on the same keep-Tanya-away-from-me theme. "Not everyone is as happy about seeing her again as you."

Meg said, "It really hurt my feelings when you called her a bitch."

My hackles shot up. "What about my feelings? What about trusting that I must have had a pretty good reason to call her that?"

For a long moment, we seemed to take each other's measure like duelers about to choose weapons. And then the defensive set of Meg's jaw softened. I could understand her not wanting to believe anything bad about her mother. She didn't want the perfect fantasy she'd created in her mind to crumble or be exposed for what it really was. A sham. "She, my mom, said you'd called her that because of the bad juju between her and Susan. I told her you wouldn't do that."

I was glad to learn Meg had defended me, but my pulse was

tripping at the possibility of learning the history between our mothers, since my family wouldn't tell me. "Did Tanya say what that bad juju was?"

Meg made a face. "She didn't volunteer anything."

And Meg hadn't asked, I realized, for fear of touching on why Tanya had abandoned her. Sympathy and disappointment twined through me, but I couldn't drop it. "I wish you would have asked. Billie and Mom are staying mum on the subject."

"Maybe it's best we don't know." I could almost see the rose-colored glasses dropping into place on her lovely face.

I hated to play devil's advocate, but someone had to. "Meg, you might not want to hear this, but you don't know Tanya. She's not the mommy you remember, the mommy you wanted her to be. You're trusting her too much too soon, believing everything she says, taking her word when she might be lying. I mean, who do you think sent the photo to Peter of you and Troy dancing?"

"Not my mom. And not me."

The glare she shot me was accusatory. I blanched at the unspoken indictment. "I didn't even take pictures last night." I slapped my phone into her hand. I was this close to telling her to leave, to deal alone with the wedding mess she'd created. The words died on my tongue as an old memory flashed, tugging me back to the saddest day of my life. My daddy's funeral. Meg finding me on the dock, holding my hand until the sun went down and we were both shivering in the chill night air. I could still hear her telling me that Daddy wouldn't have left me if he could have helped it. My throat tightened. We'd bonded that day. The glue was still tighter than any outside force, no matter how hard it pulled. "Go ahead, look. You won't find any photos from last night. Your mom was the one taking the pictures. Not me."

Meg set the phone on the coffee table without looking at it. Self-reproach shone in her eyes as she sought my gaze. "Oh God, Daryl Anne, of course you didn't do that. You wouldn't. You couldn't. I didn't mean to imply you did. I don't know what I'm thinking or why."

I could think of a reason, and her name began with a T. I didn't say it. I hated how contentious this was getting, even if we both had reason to be upset. "Well, someone did."

"The photos were sent from my phone," Meg said.

"What?"

"Yes. One minute I had it, the next, well, I lost track of it."

As usual. That meant anyone of the bachelorette party could have sent those photos to Peter. But who was most likely to have done it? Tanya was back on top of my suspect list, but she wasn't the only one. "Do you think Ash did it?"

Meg blinked. The idea had obviously not occurred to her. "Why would she?"

"I don't know. Why would anyone?" I sighed, another idea occurring to me. "Maybe Troy?"

"No," she said too quickly.

I considered asking her to pinkie swear, but I recalled the way they were together last night and wasn't as positive as Meg. "He didn't look to me like he was over you. Or like he's one bit happy about you marrying someone other than him."

Her cheeks went scarlet. "How did you know?"

I rolled my eyes. "Meg, do you still have feelings for Troy? Serious feelings?"

"No." She shook her head, her ruby curls catching flecks of sunlight, giving her an angelic look. She bit her bottom lip. "I don't know. Maybe."

Wow. Just wow. A kid caught with his hand in the cookie jar didn't look this guilty. I blurted, "Did you and Troy spend the night together?"

"No." Her eyes widened. "I wouldn't."

The tightness in my chest eased a notch. "Well, thank God for small favors."

"You didn't really think I would, did you?" She lifted the coffee cup she'd ignored until now and took a sip, peering at me over its rim.

How did I answer that? It wasn't like I didn't know their steamy history or how hard she'd taken their breakup. "Before last night, no. But after watching you two making goo-goo eyes at each other, dancing so close a piece of ribbon couldn't fit between you, well, I-I…"

I shrugged. Meg blushed again. I should have left it at that. Let her speak, but I was on a roll and couldn't seem to stop while I was ahead. "After being left at the casino, and then not hearing from you all night or half the morning, I confess, a few things were running through my imagination."

Her hand went to her mouth as if she might be sick. "I have no excuse. I got caught up. The champagne. The limo. The excitement of having my mom around. Our fight. Troy. It's like I don't know me anymore. Who am I? Why am I doing this crazy shit? I don't understand. I don't know what to think. I can't explain it."

She'd always been the Queen of Chaos. Always. It was as if the random drama she created filled the gaping crater created by her mother's abandonment. On the plus side, Meg was never dull. I tried to put myself into her shoes. What if I were as stressed as she'd been this week over the normal, last-minute wedding preparations? What if then, my former lover suddenly appeared on the eve on my wedding, acting as though he wanted to pick up where we left off? How would I feel? If it had been a love like Meg and Troy's, I'd feel pretty darned conflicted and probably confused.

Then add in the biggest stressor of all—the chance to reconnect with a mother I'd ached for half of my life. Another memory from the day of my daddy's funeral came to me. This time it was Meg telling me that her mother was never coming back, the words so full of conviction they'd chilled me. To Meg, her mother's return must feel like a miracle. She finally had that one missing element restored.

Compassion spread through me. "I'm sorry it's all so difficult, Meg. This was supposed to be the happiest time of your life."

Although tears glistened in her eyes, none fell. She inhaled a shuddery breath and spoke in a shaky voice, "Am I having fun yet?"

I took a long sip of coffee. "Did Troy and his gang go with you and the bridesmaids when you left the casino?"

She bit her lower lip and nodded, remorse projecting from every inch of her. "We went clubbing. I swear I didn't know you weren't in the limo when we left the casino."

That was probably true. I imagined the group of them crammed into that big car, champagne flowing, Troy working his magic on Meg, keeping her distracted while someone in the group used her phone to record it all and then send the images to Peter. A wayward shiver tracked down my spine.

"I didn't get my phone back until this morning," Meg said.

"Pardon?" I frowned, my mind still on suspects and motives.

"It's why I didn't answer your texts. I didn't see them until just before I saw you. The limo driver dropped the phone off at my dad's this morning. It was why I went to the café."

My heart sank. "Did your dad see the photos too?"

She made a face. "My dad hates cell phones. He refuses to own one and barely tolerates his customers using them in the café."

We both smiled. But instead of laughing, Meg let out a little sob. "Daryl Anne, please don't be mad at me. Please forgive me. I don't want to fight with you. Not ever. I swear I don't know what's wrong with me."

Tears filled her eyes, and this time they ran down her cheeks, and I realized that I was looking at her through my own tears. Mom was right. We'd been friends too long not to work out whatever might try to come between us. Even our own craziness. "I don't want to fight either."

She hugged me so tight I couldn't breathe. "I don't know what I'd do without you, Daryl Anne. You and Dad are my anchors. The only ones I can count on, and I've been a bad daughter and an awful friend. I don't even know how you got home last night."

I said, "Seth took me."

Meg released me, wiped at her tears, studying me with interest. "Seth?"

I swiped at my own damp face and smirked. "Don't go reading anything into it. He still thinks of me as a pal. Nothing more."

"Are you sure?"

I shrugged. "What does it matter? We're heading back to L.A. in a couple of days. Our love lives are a mess, but it's a good thing you and Peter called off the wedding because you shouldn't marry one man when you're still have romantic feelings for another."

"What? We didn't call off the wedding. Peter was angry but, when I told him that what went on between Troy and me last night was just some dancing and flirting, he believed me. You saw. It was all innocent."

If that was innocent, I was a monkey's uncle. Meg was in complete denial. I wanted to shake her until those rose-colored glasses shattered and she woke up from this fantasy. "How can you marry Peter when you just admitted that you might still be in love with Troy?"

"I didn't say that I was in love with Troy. Just that I was still attracted to him. It's not the same thing. I love Peter."

She looked so sincere, I decided to back off and stop challenging her. In the end, she had to do what felt right to her. Not what I felt was right for her. But was one of the duties of the maid of honor to allow the bride-to-be to marry the wrong guy? And what about the person who'd tried to ruin the wedding? What would he or she do when they discovered their nefarious plan hadn't worked?

Chapter 6

Meg and I had made amends. I should feel relief and joy as I readied for the rehearsal and dinner afterward. So why was my stomach one big knot of dread? *Someone had tried to ruin Meg's wedding, and might try again.* I stared at my reflection, frowning at what stared back. As Key Wardrobe, I prided myself on selecting the right outfit to fit the scene, but this flowery sundress with the cloth belt—that I'd bought on a whim, that I'd thought apropos for the event—made me look prepubescent and as washed of color as the day we buried my daddy.

My hands shook as I rifled through the few clothes I'd brought with me, then through the things hanging in my closet that I'd left behind when I moved to California. How desperate was that? If I didn't find something soon, I'd be late. I had an urgent sense that I shouldn't be late.

Mom peeked in. "Aren't you dressed yet?"

"I can't figure out what to wear."

"Definitely not that," she said, eyeing the fuchsia profusion with disdain. "That color does nothing for your skin tone, sweetheart."

She helped me go through my things and shook her head sadly. "None of this seems right either."

"I should have borrowed something from wardrobe," I said, sighing with regret.

"Maybe something of mine would work for you."

I winced at the suggestion. Our styles were light years apart.

She snapped her fingers. "Oh, wait a minute. I might have the perfect thing. Hang on while I get it."

Like I was going to leave in my underwear. I heard the whirr of the elevator descending to the shop and a few minutes later as it ascended. She returned with a dress covered in protective plastic draped across her arm. "Someone ordered it for an aunt of the groom, you see, and then decided it wasn't appropriate for the wedding." Mom made a face. "Or for her age, frankly."

"Do you think it will fit me?"

"It should. If you haven't lost too much weight since moving to L.A." She removed the covering, exposing a white dress with royal blue and black accents. My skin tone is winter; primary colors always flatter me. My heart raced as I slipped into it, zipping it up.

Mom said, "It's a bit loose in the waist, but if we adjust the belt a notch, like this…" She fussed over me before stepping back to let me see my reflection.

The top had a shallow V-neck and was just full enough that, with the belt tightened, you couldn't tell it wasn't a perfect fit. The heaviness weighing on my spirit seemed to lift a bit. I rotated my hips slightly and the full skirt danced around the top of my knees "I love the fabric and the little cap sleeves. It's so feminine."

I slipped into my strappy black sandals, giving myself one last glance.

"Ahh," Mom said, "look how this dress makes your eyes pop. It's like it was designed with you in mind, sweetheart. I'm glad I didn't send it back. You're going to look beautiful in all those photos Seth will be taking tonight."

Seth. My pulse skipped, and butterflies filled my stomach. The last thing I needed was to be distracted by that sexy man. Or my wayward feelings for him. What I did need, however, was to find out who was out to stop this wedding and why.

* * *

The wedding was being held at Tie the Knot, Tyson Knott's ten-acre private estate, the favorite choice of marrying couples with deep pockets. The grounds were fenced on three sides, the fourth side abutting Puget Sound. The offered venues included a ballroom wedding and reception package, a traditional non-denominational service in the large chapel with a ballroom reception afterward, a small chapel wedding with a garden reception, or a garden wedding with a garden reception.

Peter had only agreed to have the ceremony in Weddingville. And then, only the closest of friends and family had been invited to the very private nuptials. None of Peter's family were coming. His agent was doing double-duty as his best man and grooms-man. As soon as the "I do's" were said, Peter and Meg were jetting off for their honeymoon in an undisclosed location in Europe. Even Meg didn't know where. Their reception was scheduled for three months from now in the Beverly Hills mansion of a world-famous actress—his mother's best friend.

I guessed that Meg was swept up in the glamour of it all, but

I wondered how much she'd regret not having the reception in her hometown, once the glitter stopped blinding her.

The guard at the gate asked me for ID. I rolled my eyes and reminded him that he'd known me since I was in diapers, and he waved me through. The road to the parking area was tree-lined and elegant. Tents were being set up near the water's edge. I could see Zelda's crayon-yellow hair bobbing here and there among the workers as she orchestrated the tasks. The ceremony would take place tomorrow afternoon in the tent, but because the preparations were still underway, the pastor had suggested the rehearsal be held in the little chapel that overlooked the garden.

An air of serenity, beauty, and peace surrounded me as I stepped from my car. I had to admit there was something romantic and magical about this setting. I followed the path from the parking lot up the rise to the building that had stood on this spot for a hundred years, enduring wind and sun and storm, welcoming the faithful and the faithless, offering shelter and comfort, and a sense of being in a place where God would listen to your prayers and regrets without judgment.

The simple steeple seemed like a pale hand offering a cross to the heavens. I pushed inside. The outer room was little more than a foyer. A table displaying brochures with the chapel's history sat beneath a stained-glass window. Double doors opened into the nave, an area about the size of a small barn, with open-beamed rafters and a row of pews on either side of the aisle that lead to the altar. The original hardwood floors were refurbished, stained to a dark, gleaming polish, and the walls wore a fresh coat of white for the coming bridal season.

I spied Big Finn in the front row, fidgeting like a child with ADD. Peter was near the altar talking quietly with the pastor,

Reverend Bell, and his agent, Walter Fields. With stylishly cut dark hair, shrewd blue eyes, and a confident swagger, Walter had ten years on Peter and twenty pounds of muscle, defined by the cut of his suit. I pegged it as Italian, handmade, costing in the mid-three-thousand range. He wore a ring the size of those given to the NFL winners of the Super Bowl. His style reminded me of cheap gangster chic, but since he'd married the daughter of one of the most prestigious talent agents in the country, his attire was anything but bargain basement.

I noticed Ash hovering near the men. I wasn't sure why Ash was here since she wasn't part of the wedding party. But since she'd learned about someone sending those photos to Peter, she seemed to have appointed herself the wedding police. I slipped in next to Meg's dad. "Where's your daughter?"

"That's what I'd like to know. She said one of her friends was bringing her. I thought that was you."

"Nope. Probably one of the bridesmaids," I said, but I feared "the friend" was more likely to be Tanya, and I suspected Big Finn shared that suspicion. God, I hoped we were wrong. This chapel was too small for the soundstage-size tension that adding Tanya to the wedding party would cause. "What if I slip outside and give Meg a call?"

"Would you?" He pleaded, eyeing my cell phone like it was an alien ray gun.

"Sure. Be right back."

I hurried up the aisle. The bridesmaids came in as I went out. No Meg. I started toward the parking lot, but voices—whispering loudly near the edge of the big chapel caught my attention. It sounded like a heated argument. I veered toward the sound and caught a glimpse of bright red hair disappearing inside. I picked up my step. A second later, I stole into a large foyer where filtered light issued through elaborate etched-glass windows.

I waited a couple of heartbeats for my eyes to adjust. I couldn't see anyone, but I heard them just beyond where I stood, on the other side of the wall. "Don't go through with this, Meg. Look at these photos."

"Oh, my God, Troy. It was you?" Meg cried. "You sent those photos to Peter."

"What? No. No, I didn't. You sent them to me to show me that you still love me."

I heard a shocked gasp from Meg. "I didn't send them to you. Or to Peter. Someone is trying to ruin my wedding."

"Good," he said. "Because these pictures prove we belong together."

"No, they don't. Last night was nice, but it was a mistake. Nothing more than nostalgia. Closure. The good-bye we never said."

Despite Meg's denial to me, this sounded as if they had slept together last night. Had they? And if they had, what business was it of mine?

"That's bullshit," Troy said, his voice surprisingly tender. "You and I are fire and lightning. You know it's true, babe."

I heard a moan, followed by a sigh, then pure silence. My pulse skipped. If I peeked around the corner, would I find them kissing? Oh, God. I should leave before things got more intense. I backed toward the exit as a breathless moan escaped from Meg, confirming my worst fear. Guilt raced through me. I didn't mean to be eavesdropping like some voyeur. Shouldn't I make some noise? Announce my presence? Tell Meg to reconsider marrying one man when she had unresolved feelings for another?

I was pretty sure the maid of honor handbook didn't cover this situation.

I spun around and bumped into a small table, knocking it over with a clatter. Meg came rushing into the foyer, Troy right behind her. He growled, "Daryl Anne, what the hell?"

"Yeah," I said, righting the table, scowling at him. "That's what I'm wondering. What is going on with you two?"

Meg shook her head. "Nothing. I'm marrying Peter."

She stormed out.

"Not if I can help it," Troy called after her.

I stepped between Troy and the door, blocking his attempt to follow Meg. Hands on hips, I used my sternest voice, the one I reserved for egotistical actors. "Don't you dare do anything more to upset her, Troy."

If I expected him to go all badass macho on me, I was disappointed. He wasn't angry; he was heartbroken. I could see it in his eyes. "I love her, Daryl Anne. I never stopped. I wasn't going to do anything about it. Or even tell her." He waved his cell phone through the air. "But after last night, after these pictures, I can't let her walk out of my life now that she's back in it."

As sorry as I felt for him, my loyalties were with my BFF, and she'd moved on. Troy needed a reality check. "She's not back in your life. You're back in hers, and the only reason is that you both happen to be home for her wedding to someone else."

"It's fate," he insisted. "Her mother said that Meg and I should—" He stopped, something dawning on him. "Tanya lied?"

"Duh?" But as images of Troy and Meg dancing flashed to mind, I understood his confusion, his frustration.

Troy groaned. "I should have known better than to believe that bitch."

I couldn't agree more, but rubbing salt into his wound didn't seem wise or kind. "What I don't understand, Troy, is why you gave Meg's mom the time of day considering how you've always felt about her. Or for that matter, what possessed you to hook up with her and go to the casino."

"Because, because..." He glanced away, unwilling to say anything that made him seem more foolish, but I knew the reason without him admitting it. Tanya had told him what he wanted to hear about Meg. And Meg's reaction to him last night had obviously confirmed that for him. My pity for the guy grew tenfold.

Troy groaned. "I swear that bitch is going to pay for everything she's done to Meg. And to me." The venom in his voice had me shrinking from him. Ice layered my veins.

Troy left me standing there, awful scenarios of what he meant to do to Tanya running through my imagination. I reminded myself that he was a police officer, sworn to uphold the law, and that he had always been the guy to follow the rules. He wasn't going to do anything to jeopardize that. Nothing that I should worry about, right?

And yet, I did worry every step of the path back to the small chapel. A murmur of voices inside the nave stopped when I entered. "Ah, there you are, Daryl Anne," Reverend Bell said. "Now we can begin."

I didn't want to begin. I wanted a few minutes alone with Meg. She needed to be honest about her feelings for Troy. To me. To herself. If there was even the slightest possibility that Troy was right about how she felt about him, then it had to be addressed, before she married Peter.

Frankly, I didn't see what Meg saw in Peter. Yes, he was handsome, and rich, and famous, and dressed well, and...and...

Nope, that was all I had. If you can't say something nice about someone and all that. To me, his bad attributes outweighed his good ones, but maybe I wasn't being fair to Peter. Maybe he just wasn't my type.

Reverend Bell made us take our respective places. That meant Big Finn and Meg were right behind me. No way to talk to her now. But the moment Meg reached the altar, Peter laid claim to her. I couldn't even catch her eye. He hugged her to his side as if she might disappear if he weren't touching her. Would she? Was the thought of running off with Troy circulating through her chaotic brain? The crease between her eyebrows indicated an inner turmoil of some sort, but it might be as simple as fretting that Troy would do something rash, like speaking up instead of forever holding his peace.

I had a vision of that scene in *The Graduate* when Dustin Hoffman interrupts the wedding and runs off with the bride, played by Katharine Ross. My last nerve frayed, and I felt a laugh burbling to the surface. I swallowed hard, fearing one laugh would lead to another and another until someone had to slap me. *Calm down, Daryl Anne. Stop letting your imagination rule your good sense. Think this through.*

I took a couple of deep breaths. It seemed to clear the fuzz from my brain. Troy wasn't behind the Instagrammed photos; he hadn't been trying to stop the wedding. Whoever was, however, had manipulated the situation between Troy and Meg, likely counting on it to light the fuse that would dynamite the wedding. Tanya? Or someone in the chapel right now? Gooseflesh crawled over me, my gaze flicking from one person to the next.

When I'd agreed to be the maid of honor, I hadn't known all that position required. So I'd done my homework, read books and researched online sites. Not one of those sources mentioned anything about the maid of honor also needing to be a private investigator. But if this wedding was to come off without another hitch, I needed to find the evildoer and stop him, or her, in their devious tracks. Before tomorrow. *How was I supposed to do that?*

Chapter 7

The rehearsal dinner was being held at Celebration, a five-star restaurant that sat on the water's edge. The current owners, Mick and Vick Martino had renovated it from top to bottom, turning this once fish processing plant into a gourmand's delight that dished up some of the best seafood in the Pacific Northwest. Walking in, I was assailed by the aromas. Vick directed me to the elegant private dining room with its sweeping views of Puget Sound and Mount Rainier in the distance.

I arrived to find Zelda fussing over the place settings, and the flowers, and orchestrating the setup of the hors d'oeuvre table as if this was the restaurant's first event dinner. As usual, she was a rainbow of colors, topped by her crayon-yellow bob. She spied me and waved me over. "Whaddya think?"

I feasted my eyes on the Russian caviar, giant prawns, and smoked salmon nestled in a bed of chipped ice. Cheese slices, delicate crackers, and some kind of creamy dip accompanied the offerings. "Nice."

"Peter Wolfe had the caviar flown in from Russia. Flown. In." Despite her years of experience as a wedding planner, Zelda seemed unable to imagine actually knowing someone who was this extravagant. Her eyes took on a dreamy look. "Meg's life is going to be a lot different after tomorrow."

"It is," I said, uncertain if the wedding was actually going to take place given all the undercurrents rocking the boat. But I had no idea, then, just how hard those undercurrents were or how different Meg's life was about to become.

My mother's advice sounded in my head. *This is supposed to be fun.* Although I found a smile, my rattled nerves refused to join in my attempt at revelry. Thinking some liquid encouragement might help, I glanced longingly toward the complimentary bar being stocked with ice, liquor, and glasses on the end wall.

"I'm so sorry for being late," a woman called to Zelda as she hurried into the room. She was willowy in a long, flowery dress, her chestnut hair wound into a braid atop her head. "I had car trouble."

"You're not late," Zelda assured her. "Just on time. We have you set up over here."

The harpist Peter had hired to play background music throughout the dinner, I realized. Zelda directed her to the chair and harp sitting directly opposite the bar. I turned my gaze to the rest of the room, noting the gold and silver party decorations. One long table had been set in the center of the room, draped with a white cloth and a silver overlay; the floral arrangements were white roses, baby's breath, and gold ribbons. The silverware was gold, the dishes white with gold trim, the napkins silver. I recognized Peter's touch without anything of Meg's. It was more Hollywood than Weddingville, more formal than festive. Was this what her life with Peter would be? All about him?

"A penny for your thoughts," someone said near my ear, causing me to flinch. But I recognized that sexy alto and exhaled. Seth Quinlan. And now a genuine smile filled me, spreading through me.

"If that's the only pickup line you've got, Quinlan, I don't expect you're doing all that well with the ladies," I teased, turning toward him, my breath catching at how handsome he was in a white dress shirt and trousers, his tawny hair slightly mussed, his warm brown eyes smiling.

He grinned, and my toes curled. "You seem pretty preoccupied with my love life, Blessing."

I blushed. "No, I…" A clever comeback failed me. I cleared my throat, my gaze locked on his sexy mouth, my thoughts going places that were clearly inappropriate given where we were, why we were here, and his disinterest in me. I gave myself a mental shake, switching the conversation to safer territory. "Thank you for last night, for rescuing me."

"Yep, I'm a regular knight in shining armor." He glanced around, then settled that compelling gaze on me, studying me as he might a subject he wanted to photograph. "I'm guessing you and Meg worked things out?"

"We did." He'd been so easy to talk with last night, to confide in. Could I tell him what I'd discovered—that someone was trying to derail the wedding? Maybe he could help figure out who. The obvious suspect was Tanya, and yet that seemed too obvious. And biased. My dislike of her didn't make her guilty. Besides, I just couldn't fathom why she'd come back into Meg's life after all these years, claiming to want to make up for the past, while actually intending to hurt Meg again.

"I'm glad you and Meg made up, but you don't seem exactly happy. Troubled, yes, gleeful, no."

"So you do read minds for loose change."

"I read faces, for free," he said, raising his camera and snapping my photo before I could protest. He kept the camera to his eye, studying me through the lens. "Yep. There is definitely something worrying you. If you want to share, I'm a good listener."

I considered, then decided this wasn't the time or the place. "As much as I'd like to take your penny, my thoughts are best left unshared. For now."

"Later then, but if you change your mind…" His warm gaze stroked my face. "You know where to find me."

I grinned as something sweet cut into my sour mood. This was feeling too cozy and comfy. Too dangerous. Seth didn't seem to notice. He was checking out the decorations, the lighting, lifting his camera, adjusting the lens. A thought popped into my mind. "You were told that Peter and Meg want the rehearsal dinner photos to seem as if they were taken by friends and family, right?

"Yep. Nothing as formal as the wedding shots they want taken tomorrow." He quirked an eyebrow. "Might as well give out those little throwaway cameras."

"Oh, no. Peter's not letting anyone take unauthorized photos. In fact, he wants all cell phones checked at the door." I held out my hand. "I'll need yours now, please."

Seth lowered his camera. "It's in my car."

"Really?"

"You can search me, if you don't believe me, Blessing." To my surprise, he held his arms out, looking like he'd enjoy being frisked by me. He had no idea how much I would enjoy it. When I stepped back, he chuckled. "Chicken."

"Be careful what you dare me to do, Quinlan. You might recall the time you dared me to push you off the big dock."

"Always more devil than angel." He chuckled a little deeper. "But I shouldn't have to remind you that this isn't the first celebrity wedding I've photographed."

"Sorry. For a moment there, I forgot to whom I was speaking." Neither Seth nor I had gone to college to earn degrees for our current professions. We'd learned and honed our crafts the old-fashioned way, apprenticing at our parents' and grandparents' knees. He'd had a camera in his hand by the time he was four. His grandfather had photographed mayors and governors, his father Kurt Cobain and Bill Gates.

"Things weren't so bad in my dad's day." Seth's teasing smile had gone into hiding. "Can't blame a celebrity these days for being paranoid about unwanted photos that are open to mis-interpretation getting into the press. It's rampant. I always leave my phone locked in my car when I'm on a job. I never want to be accused of offering pictures to the media. My business would tank if my professionalism were compromised like that."

I sighed. "Makes me glad that I work behind the scenes. No one cares who I am." An awful thought occurred to me of one more way that Meg's life would be different after tomorrow. "Meg is about to lose that anonymity, isn't she?"

"Yep. Paparazzi staking out Peter will soon recognize her. Her car. She'll be followed everywhere. The more famous Peter becomes, the more she'll struggle to avoid the press."

"And the more she gives up in order to avoid them, the smaller her world will become." The realization sent an ache of sadness through me for Meg. She was a small-town girl with a penchant for chaos and a perpetual need to be loved. She was unlikely to realize the inherent danger of the press until it was too late. I groaned. "Why couldn't she have fallen for one of the key grips or set designers? Why the star of the show?"

Seth made a face. "That's the problem with love. The heart wants who it wants. And that's not always the person who is best for us."

"Speaking from experience, Quinlan?" I tried reading his face, but he wasn't giving anything away.

"Just an observation."

I didn't believe him, but the bartender was ready to serve, and I was ready to drink. Beyond ready. "Well, I'll let you do your thing. I'm off to play phone police. Have to make sure the staff and the harpist aren't carrying."

Seth laughed as I strode off. Hearing the click of his camera, I wondered if he was taking a sweeping shot of the room or a shot of me walking away. I didn't look back. After securing a glass of wine and speaking to both the bartender and harpist, I learned that Mick and Vick were playing phone valets tonight. I was relieved not to have the responsibility. I returned to the long table to set the bridesmaids' gifts next to the appropriate place cards on the table.

Zelda appeared at my side to remind me to keep Tanya in check, and I reassured her that I'd do my best. The bridesmaids and their plus ones arrived, laughing and jovial. The three men went straight to the bar while the women found their seats at the table, chattering gaily.

Zelda had grabbed a glass of white wine, I noticed, as she returned to my side. "So how did the rehearsal go?"

I sipped my merlot. "Tanya wasn't there, if that's what you're wondering."

Tension seemed to float off her, softening her sweet features and bringing a smile to her eyes. "Dare I hope that she won't show tonight either?"

But as the words left her mouth, I saw her gaze dart to the

doorway behind me, and her face went dark. Sure enough, as I glanced around, Tanya and Kramer were coming in. He was dressed in khakis and a polo shirt, no socks. He seemed ill at ease. Out of his element.

She, however, wore an air of entitlement, punctuated by a hot-red dress that left nothing to the imagination. And yet, several men in the room seemed to be imagining plenty. I thought the bartender's eyes were going to pop out of their sockets, and the harpist missed a chord.

And out of the mouth of the woman dressed like a piñata came, "Where'd she get that? Hoochie Mamas R Us?"

I choked on my wine. I'd been thinking updated Sharon Stone in *Basic Instinct*. Zelda patted my back. Before I could recover, Seth, shining knight and diplomat, stepped up, taking a couple of shots of Tanya and Kramer and then inviting them to collect drinks and indulge in the appetizers. Where were Peter and Meg? Why were we greeting *their* guests? They should have been here first. Before me. The only responsibility I had tonight as the maid of honor was to see that the bridesmaids' gifts were distributed. *Check. Done.* Nothing in my handbook said "play hostess at rehearsal dinner."

"Can't tell you how relieved I am that Peter isn't allowing cell phones during the party tonight," Ash said, arriving a bit breathless as if she'd been running "No one is going to ruin this wedding if I can help it."

I asked if she'd heard from Meg since the rehearsal, but she hadn't. "You know Peter. He likes to make an entrance."

Ash headed to the bar as Reverend Bell and his wife arrived. I took a minute to ask him if Meg or Peter had mentioned making a stop along the way, but he shook his head, claiming he hadn't heard anything. I considered going out front and using the restaurant phone to call Meg, but froze in place as the next guest arrived.

Big Finn lumbered in, tie askew, brows furrowed, lips pressed so tight that air couldn't slip through them. His jovial father-of-the-bride spirits seemed as absent as his daughter. The tension in the room vibrated against the walls, twanging through me as if I were a harp string. He didn't acknowledge me or answer whether he knew Meg and Peter's whereabouts. His gaze skipped over me, then over Zelda, and slammed into Tanya. Not a speck of male appreciation or lust appeared. Just the cold stare one gave a poisonous spider before squashing it.

I gulped wine and spun back toward the entrance, hoping to catch sight of Meg and Peter. Instead, the couple coming toward me took me by surprise.

"Oh, darling, there you are," my mother said, wearing the fuchsia sundress that washed me out, but complemented her auburn hair and creamy skin perfectly. I gaped, head quirked to one side as if I were staring at a mirage, trying to discern whether or not my eyes were deceiving me. Hadn't Mom told me a couple of hours ago that she and Billie weren't coming tonight? Yes she had. They both had. But here they were—as welcome and lovely as a pair of spring flowers, smiling brightly. My insides warmed. It was such a nice, unexpected twist in a day full of wrong turns.

I grinned and hugged my mother. "Thought you wouldn't step foot in this place if *that woman* was here." I kept my voice low enough for only her and Billie to hear.

Gram sniffed. "I reminded Susan that Meg is like a second daughter to her and granddaughter to me and letting *that woman* keep us from helping our Meg celebrate the happiest event of her life is just plain wrong."

Mom retied the long fabric belt and grinned. "Sometimes your gram makes a whole lot of sense."

"Most of the time." Gram sniffed.

Mom leaned back and offered me a wink and then plucked at my hair. I sensed she was a second away from licking her finger and smoothing my eyebrows. I released her and stepped out of reach.

Mom said, "I realized I didn't want to miss Meg's party. I mean, since there's to be no reception tomorrow after the wedding, this might be our only chance to offer her our blessings."

"I'm so glad you're both here."

"Rites of passage should be celebrated," Billie said.

"With those who love you," Mom added. "Those you love."

"Meg will be thrilled."

"Where is she?" Billie asked, peering down her nose at the small groups clustered about the room. "Meg, I mean."

Ah, the question of the hour. "I have no idea. I can't text her since I don't have my phone, but I assume they're on their way or they'd have called the restaurant."

"Of course," Mom said as she pretended she wasn't trying to spot Tanya.

"Rude, if you ask me," Billie said. "Finn taught her better manners than that. Must be the Hollywood influence."

I opened my mouth to defend L.A., but then I realized she might be right. Although I was disinclined to blame the industry. More likely Peter's influence.

Mom shushed Gram and led her to the bar. I had to find Zelda about fitting Mom and Gram into the table configuration—after having had her remove them less than an hour ago. And remind her that they also wanted to sit as far from Tanya as possible. I had a mental flash of the table listing to one side like a ship from the weight of all those preferring not to sit near Meg's mom.

Zelda squeezed Gram and Mom in beside Finn and herself. For the next half hour, Zelda and I worked the room, both of us avoiding Tanya. Big Finn kept his distance too, holding a drink, standing in a corner, his gaze never leaving his ex-wife. She didn't seem unnerved by his stare, but I would have been.

Where were Meg and Peter?

I'd about made up my mind to make that phone call when they finally showed up with Walter Fields in tow. A cheer greeted them. Meg smiled her brightest smile as Peter offered apologies, stating that he and his agent had to deal with a movie offer that came in out of the blue. It was a chance he couldn't pass up, but please don't ask for details as he wasn't able to discuss those until the deal was inked. I studied Meg. Her smiles were as fake as that excuse. There hadn't been an urgent movie offer. Peter just liked making an entrance.

"Get used to it," I whispered to her, handing her a glass of wine. "He can't help himself. Diva."

This made her laugh. "I know, I know."

I stood aside as Meg made up for lost time, mingling and apologizing to her guests for being late. I tried to relax, but the undercurrent that had my nerves on edge earlier returned, a nagging ache just below my breastbone. Something bad was coming. I prayed I was overreacting. Or wrong. The sensation lingered, and with every passing minute, my dread increased.

"Vick says it's time to start serving," Zelda told me. "Would you help me spread the word? I don't want to just shout it out."

"Sure." But she was doing a great job herding the guests to the table so I decided to slip into the ladies' room before getting settled. When I came out, I heard a couple of voices around the corner by the men's room. I went to check, but halted in my tracks when I recognized Peter's voice. I was so used to hearing it on set that I'd know it anywhere. He was clearly pissed off, telling someone, "If you say one word about that to Meg, I'll kill you."

Chapter 8

Originally, I was to sit beside Meg, but Tanya had switched her place card with mine. I found myself in the middle of the table, seated next to Kramer. He looked as unhappy about it as I was. As I sat, he handed me a small envelope with my name scrawled on it. "TR said this was tucked into your napkin."

I scowled at the envelope, my annoyance about to boil over. It was small and square like a thank-you note. As curious as I was, I wasn't about to read it with Kramer's curious gaze studying me. I stuffed it into a pocket of my dress to deal with at a later time when I wasn't rattled by overheard death threats. I stole covert glances at Meg's fiancé. Who had he warned? What secret was he keeping from Meg? *Something bad enough to threaten murder.*

I shuddered at the thought as my conscience deliberated what I should do about it. Tell Meg and let her decide whether or not to pursue it? I glanced at my best friend, watching her nibbling her bottom lip, a sign that she was still struggling with unresolved feelings, and I knew I couldn't give her one more thing to try to figure out before tomorrow. I should either confront Peter with what I'd heard and demand an explanation or let it drop.

"If you say one word about that to Meg, I'll kill you."

I shuddered again. I couldn't pretend I hadn't heard it, and I couldn't drop it.

Peter stood, clinking his spoon against the side of his water glass. Silence hummed across the table, conversations stopped, and silverware was set aside. All eyes focused on Peter. He was in his element, TV star, movie actor, playing the lead role with a script written just for him, to an audience of adoring fans. *Cue that famous smile.*

I watched the bridesmaids turn to putty and marveled that Mom and Billie were also being sucked in. Even Ash. Only Kramer, Big Finn, and I seemed immune to his spell. But then, Finn wasn't paying attention. He hadn't taken his eyes off his ex, that gaze more hate-filled than ever. I guessed Tanya stealing my seat next to Meg had stirred his temper more. Salt rubbed in old wounds. Meg would have preferred both her parents sit near her, but Finn had vetoed that, choosing the opposite end of the table and being as withdrawn as a turtle into its shell.

When I reached for my wine, my gaze landed on Tanya. She was staring at her future son-in-law intently. I'd watched Meg introduce Peter to her earlier, and for an actor with his range, he'd seemed unable to put on the glad-to-meet-you warmth that I knew Meg craved. In my opinion, it was a point in his favor. There was that odd gleam in Tanya's eye, the one she'd had when she told Peter, "Surprise." It was a gotcha look. What trouble was she plotting now? I also noticed Peter was avoiding her gaze. Was it Tanya he'd threatened earlier?

Peter interrupted my thoughts. "I want to welcome you all and apologize again for our late arrival. We appreciate that you're all complying with our 'no cell phones or cameras' request and apologize for the inconvenience."

He took a sip from his cocktail. "Same rule applies tomorrow too. Sorry folks, but we hope you'll understand. We don't want our special day plastered all over the tabloids." Although he hadn't even glanced her way, Tanya reacted as if Peter had been speaking directly to Kramer and her. The look wasn't lost on Ash, I observed. If her expression was any indication, she was mentally writing Tanya a wedding police ticket.

Tanya stood, smiled sweetly, her drink raised in a toast, and her gaze going first to Peter, then to Big Finn. "*I* wouldn't do anything to ruin my daughter's wedding."

The words send a strange chill through me, like a foreboding.

A bear-like growl escaped Big Finn, his face twisted in a thunderous scowl. I braced for an explosion of temper, but Zelda tugged on his sleeve, getting through to him. He nodded, settled down, and picked up his soup spoon again.

Peter directed everyone to dig in and enjoy.

It was a five-course, plated dinner, each dish more exquisite than the last, but the salad had barely been served when it was blatantly obvious that the groom had little in common with anyone else at the table. His ability to engage in small talk apparently required a script. He chatted with his Walter and Ash, who were seated on his left, totally ignoring his fiancée and her mother on his right, the other guests in the middle of the table, the bridesmaids, and his future father-in-law.

I noticed a telltale shake in his right hand as he picked at his salad. He startled whenever he heard the click of Seth's camera, his gaze darting over the guests and staff in search of a smuggled-in cell phone, a hidden camera. I'd never seen him so jumpy. Pre-wedding jitters? Or secrets he'd kill to keep secret?

But he wasn't my only concern. Given Big Finn's mood, I prayed Mom and Gram knew better than to mention that Tanya had crashed the bachelorette party and that Meg and I had had a fight because of it. I was too far away to hear their conversation, but the irritated twitching of Big Finn's eyebrows wasn't reassuring.

I concentrated on my meal. Each plate set before me was like an artist's rendering in food, every bite a taste bud delight. The portions, however, reminded me of those served in a French restaurant I splurged on a couple of times a year. Small, but calorie laden. Just as well that my stomach was in such turmoil that I could eat little of all five courses. If this kept up, I'd have an ulcer before Meg and Peter left for their honeymoon. But at least I wouldn't gain any weight.

"Look at her." Kramer nudged his elbow into my side, startling me out of my dark thoughts. I'd forgotten he was seated on my left. He'd been silent throughout the first four courses of the meal. I glanced toward him, trying to connect his comment with someone at the table. His gaze was shooting daggers at Tanya. "Someone could drown in her bullshit."

Tanya had her blond head tilted toward Meg. Ash was watching mother and daughter like a hawk. Whatever Tanya was saying had my best friend's eyes full of joy. I prayed Kramer was wrong. That Tanya wasn't spewing a stream of lies. But I had no reason to believe otherwise.

"Makes me sick." Kramer shoved his dessert away, nose wrinkled, as if the chocolate mousse were a mound of dog poo. "Never even mentioned she had a daughter until she realized who her kid was marrying, and even then, she kept the guy's identity secret from me. Peter Fucking Wolfe."

"Really. You can't guess why she didn't tell you?" I asked,

possibilities tripping through my mind, but I suggested the one that seemed most likely to me. "Was she, perhaps, afraid you'd spill all the details of the wedding to the highest paying gossip site?"

I swear he turned the color of eggplant, his eyes narrowing into slits, but he didn't miss a beat. "What makes you think I haven't?"

For a second, I went very still. After thinking it through, though, I shook my head. "I doubt it very much. After all, you and Tanya are the only two members of the media in town. You'd be the most likely suspects. And believe me, Peter would see to it that you were both fired."

Kramer zinged a glance at Peter, his lip curling. He muttered, "That asshole. Thinks he can get away with anything. Him and that agent. To them, I don't exist. Their mistake."

What did that mean? I considered how to ask him to explain, but Kramer was back to glaring at Tanya. "You'd think she was running for mother-of-the-fucking-year."

"You don't think it's natural for a mother to want to be part of her daughter's wedding?"

"Hah."

Yeah, me either. Not this mother.

Kramer said, "TR doesn't have a single speck of maternal instinct. Trust me. She was hiding behind the door when God handed out that particular gene."

"Then why did she even seek to reconnect with Meg?"

"Him." Kramer nodded toward Peter.

A sinking feeling slipped through me. It was what I'd expected. I offered the reason I'd come up with. "She thinks her daughter being married to a rich, famous actor will open doors for her, doesn't she?"

"Hell no. She just wants to reconnect with him."

Reconnect? The bottom fell out of my stomach. "She used to date Peter?"

"If you're using *date* as a euphemism, then yes."

My eyes opened so wide they hurt. "What! When?"

"That's for me to know and you to wonder about." Kramer scooted his chair back and headed to the bar, leaving me sitting there stunned into silence, my mind awash with slimy thoughts. Peter had slept with Tanya and was now marrying her daughter? Eww. Was it true? Shouldn't Meg be told? Could I have this information and not tell her? Oh, God. The room suddenly felt like an oven. I needed to splash cold water on my overheated face. Now.

As I headed to the ladies, I spied Seth watching me. I hoped I didn't look as ill as I felt, hoped he wouldn't follow me to offer to buy my thoughts. I might just sell them to him. Or break down and cry on those solid shoulders of his.

Luckily, I had the bathroom to myself. Everyone else seemed to still be enjoying dessert. I was wishing I'd skipped mine. I daubed a wet paper towel against my hot cheeks, mindful of my makeup. I didn't want to have to explain mascara streaks under my eyes.

The outside door opened, and a flash of red caught my eye. Tanya. I began to shake inside, as if my emotions had been put into a blender and turned to *whip*. But as stirred up as I was, I couldn't bring myself to ask her if she and Peter were once lovers. *"Don't borrow trouble,"* Billie always said.

I didn't have to mention a rumor or gossip to Meg, but once I'd confirmed something as serious as this, my options would narrow into intolerable choices. My head began to ache. I kept to a safer subject. "What's the deal between you and my mother?"

Tanya fussed with her lipstick, one eyebrow shooting up at my question. She replaced the lid on the tube of gloss, then glanced around as if to make sure we were alone. The stall doors hung open. Empty. I assured her, "No one but you and me."

She gave me her full attention, but I didn't like the reluctance in her expression. "What did Susan say it was?"

Nothing. I bit down my frustration. This was going to require another approach, but since strangling the truth out of her wasn't a good idea, I strove to be tactful. "I'd like to hear your side of it."

She seemed about to laugh. "You're offering me the benefit of the doubt?"

"Yes. For Meg's sake." I offered a smile, reining in my escalating temper and swallowing a lump of anger the size of a pincushion. "I think she would appreciate it if you and I could at least be civil."

Tanya's narrowed eyes were full of distrust. "Okay."

I didn't trust her either. But it occurred to me that, at some point, I was going to have to come to terms with her role in my best friend's life. Like it or not. I didn't much like it. I also didn't like asking her for information that I should have gotten from my mother. But my need-to-know was consuming me.

"Well," I said, encouraging her to get on with it. I realized that my body language might give away the disgust I fought to conceal and forced my arms to my sides.

Tanya leaned against the counter, arms folded, defensive. "You grew up in Weddingville. Born and raised, as they say. So I doubt you can comprehend how very unwelcoming a small town can be to newcomers."

There was a trace of bitterness in every word that painted a visual I didn't care for. I felt as though Tanya had grabbed me by the shoulders, forcing me to give her my full attention. I couldn't look away. She said, "When Finn bought the café, he had such hopes for our life here. He'd sunk every penny we had into the move. I was less enamored. It seemed like we'd arrived at the end of the world. Weddingville wasn't the bustling concern then that it is now."

She glanced toward the mirror, finger-lifting her hair as if the distraction could further distance her from the past. "The café was not an instant success. The first three weeks? Not one customer. Do have any idea the daily cost, the wasted food, the loss in revenue? Not to mention how it makes you feel?"

She didn't wait for me to answer. "Every day more wasted food. More and more. Our nest egg slipping through our fingers. Every day watching the door, seeing people walking past, peering in, raising our hopes. No one coming in. Do you know how it feels to watch your life failing right before your eyes and there's nothing you can do to stop it? On the fourth week, we had two customers. Out-of-towners."

Shame filled me. I'd always thought of my hometown as the friendliest place on Earth, where strangers and outsiders supplied our very survival. Hurt balled in my chest. Despite my personal feelings for this woman, my empathy was off the charts. I'd felt something similar when I'd moved to Los Angeles. On the outside, looking in. Off my game. As if I'd never fit in.

"Then one day, a Wednesday I recall, *he* walked in. The mayor. Daryl Blessing. Your daddy sat right at the counter where everyone passing by could see him, and he ordered the biggest breakfast on the menu. After that, a few others decided to give us a try, and soon, word of mouth got around that we had great food at reasonable prices. Daryl saved us. He was an incredible man, an amazing friend."

I couldn't speak. My worries about mascara smears fled as tears slipped from my eyes. My dad had been one of the good guys. I had so many sweet memories of his generous heart, but this was one more I would cherish.

"Eventually, he brought your mother and you around. You and Meg were the same age and hit it off right away. It seemed like we'd all be great friends. But soon I got the impression that Susan was jealous of me, the way I dressed, the way men looked at me...I'm not sure. Something. Maybe she thought Daryl paid too much attention to me."

Her words were like stones pelting into me, smashing my empathy, shattering the sweet memories of a moment ago. Exposing a rotted center. Had my dad and her...? No. No frickin' way. My memories of my parents were solid and clear. They were always kissing and holding hands and laughing together. I stopped just short of calling Tanya the *B* word again.

My face must have given me away. Tanya laughed. "You didn't ask Susan, did you?"

"I did." *She just wouldn't tell me.* Which didn't necessarily mean there was any truth in what Tanya had suggested. Did it? "She has a different version."

"I'll just bet. I think your granny was the real culprit though. She didn't like me. Thought I was too friendly with her dear son. She probably planted a bug in Susan's ear, stirred up the green-eyed monster with gossip that had no foundation."

I weighed what she'd told me. Was it the truth? Or a lie with some basis of truth? I had no way to judge.

"You look so much like your daddy, Daryl Anne. Makes me sentimental. He was a hell a man."

I sensed someone else had slipped into the ladies room. I glanced up to see my mother standing there, her face crimson, her eyes burning with hatred. She hissed, "How dare you suggest those things to my daughter about her father?"

Tanya's shoulders squared, and she spun toward my mother, a smirk on her face. "She's not a child any longer, Susan. You can't protect her from the truth forever. Besides, I sugar-coated it."

"Come on Daryl Anne," Mom reached for me, but my feet were frozen, my tongue stuck to the roof of my mouth.

"So you'd rather keep running from the truth, Susan? It's been fifteen years. Why don't you face it? If you'd given Daryl the divorce, he'd still be—"

Mom's face went ashen. Her hand flew out like a whip connecting with Tanya's cheek and rocking Tanya sideways. "Shut up. Or I swear I'll, I'll—"

"What?" Tanya reached up to touch her reddened face, but she didn't back down. Her taunt came on a laugh. "You'll kill me?"

My mother's mouth snapped open, then shut. She was shaking all over. While I felt as if I'd been zapped into a concrete statue, paralyzed by the word *divorce*. By the unspoken suggestion that my father's death was somehow connected to the hatred my mother felt for Tanya. By my mother's rare show of violence.

But Mom seemed to call on some inner calm that I couldn't even imagine she possessed. The soft words that spilled from her were more chilling than her fury had been. "Whatever I do, you won't see it coming."

Tanya blinked. Mom left without another word, without looking at me. Tanya wasn't as kind. She took one more potshot. "That's right, Daryl Anne. Your daddy was going to leave Susan for me."

Sensation returned, tingling my chilled flesh with burning pinpricks while something hot and sick danced in my stomach. I don't think I've ever hated anyone as much as I did her at that moment. If a weapon had been within my reach just then, she'd be lying on the floor bleeding.

Chapter 9

There you are." Meg caught me in a hug the second I reentered the banquet room. I clung to her much as I had the day of my father's funeral. God, how I needed her at that moment. It was as if she sensed it. She was the only one I wanted to tell what had happened, what I had just learned from our mothers. But of all people, how could I tell her? The realization sent the brittle sensation from my knees to the rest of my joints, leaving me feeling as fragile as an ancient vase. One bump and I might shatter.

Maybe I should blame Meg for bringing her mother to town, for bringing on this awful string of events. But the only thing keeping me from falling over the edge of sanity was our friendship. And how could she know the harm simply wanting her mother at her wedding would do? My gaze went to Tanya. She stood near the bar, flirting with Walter as he waited for the bartender to finish fixing his drink. She stroked his tie, and Walter looked more like she'd tightened it around his throat. He seemed to be fighting the urge to shove her away.

Meg eased back, studying me, giving me time to recall my own struggles with Tanya. I tried to hide my distress, but it caught her attention. She asked, "What's wrong?"

Damn my inability to conceal what I was thinking. One look at my face and everyone with working vision could read me like a book. "I, er, ate something that didn't agree with me."

"Oh, I'm sorry. Was it the shrimp? I thought it tasted a bit wonky."

"Probably." There. I'd given myself the perfect excuse to leave. To go home and confront my mother for answers. I gave Meg another squeeze. Why wasn't I heading to the door? The distasteful reason wormed through me. I was a coward. I didn't want to hear that Tanya had been telling me the truth, that my beloved dad had planned to leave us and run off with her. That everything I'd ever believed about my parents' relationship was a lie. I wanted to be the jolly maid of honor Meg expected, but if my fears were confirmed, I'd be hard pressed to find a smile.

A roar tore through my thoughts. Meg and I, along with everyone else in the room, froze, our collective gazes riveting on Big Finn. "I should've wrung your neck twelve years ago."

Onlookers gasped. I felt Meg go stone-still. Her cheeks flamed, but her mouth was ringed in white. I grasped her hand as if we were eleven again, the past rearing up to catapult us back in time. Two little girls holding on to each other to outride a tumultuous storm.

Tanya tossed her head and laughed, aware of the audience but apparently not smart enough to realize the danger of egging on her furious ex. "All I said was that you're more handsome than ever, Finn. Most men would be flattered."

Finn brought to mind a bull about to charge. His nostrils flared as he took a step toward her. No one moved. Meg's complexion paled and tears shone in her eyes. Pity welled in me. *I know, I know.* Meg had brought this on herself by inviting her mother to the wedding, but I couldn't help feeling bad for her. *This is supposed to be a happy time.* And in her excitement over reestablishing a lost relationship, she hadn't thought about possible consequences. Long or short term. I wanted to shout at her parents that this was not the time or place, but the words choked in my throat.

Seth, however, set his camera on the nearest table and rushed to intervene. He kept his voice low, but the room was as silent as a morgue and his words were not lost on anyone. "Do you think the two of you could set aside your differences and remember that you're here to celebrate the marriage of your daughter? This is a special night for her. Would you like her to recall it forever as the evening her parents embarrassed her in front of her friends and fiancé?"

Big Finn glanced toward Meg and blanched, his chest deflating like a spent balloon. He retreated and let Zelda lead him back to his seat. A murmur went through the guests. Seth signaled the harpist to play. Realizing the excitement was over, everyone returned to whatever they'd been doing before the disruption. Some were finishing their drinks while others were readying to leave. Only then did Tanya react. Instead of offering Meg an apology, she shrugged with an innocence I couldn't believe and mouthed an "I was trying to be nice."

Apparently, the ploy worked. Meg wasted no time joining her.

I stood where I was, total disbelief sifting through me. But I wasn't the only one. Ash leaned against her chair, staring after Tanya, her mouth twisted in a sneer.

"I was about to send someone into the ladies to make sure you were okay," Seth said, standing close to my ear. I'd been so lost in murderous thoughts that I hadn't heard or felt his approach. The warmth in his smile chased off a lingering shakiness. If I wasn't careful, I could fall hard for this knight-in-shining-armor side of Seth.

But it was my damsel-in-need-of-rescuing side that galled me. It felt like I'd lost control of my life. I loathed the feeling. I mumbled a *thank you*, hoping my complexion didn't still have that green-around-the-gills glow. Just in case it did, I added, "Something didn't agree with me."

"I can guess," he said, gesturing toward Tanya and Meg, who now huddled together like conspirators plotting a war move.

"No, you can't." Not even close. I scanned the banquet room, but there was no sign of my mom or Billie.

"They left a while ago," Seth said, convincing me that I'd too quickly dismissed his ability to guess. The man was a regular mind-reader. "Your mom also looked like something hadn't agreed with her."

"You were right," I said, giving it up. "More like *someone*."

I tried to hide my disappointment, but doubted my success. I was tired of Mom running out and avoiding my questions about Tanya, which only lent more credence to the nasty allegations. Why was I so afraid to hear the truth? What difference would it make now? None. *Let Mom cool down*. I needed to do the same. It occurred to me then that maybe Mom had left in a rush to avoid doing bodily harm to Tanya. The same bodily harm I wanted to do to Meg's mom.

"Yeah," Seth said, lifting his camera, the lens pointed toward the lady in red. "I've been asking myself why a woman would come to her long-lost daughter's wedding only to stir up a lot of trouble and unhappiness."

"Yeah, first she brings Troy to the bachelorette party, then she takes suggestive photos of them dancing, that got sent to Peter, by the way."

"Jesus." Seth's camera came away from his eye.

"It caused quite a stir." And he didn't know the trouble she'd tried stirring up in the restroom. I stifled a shudder. "Kramer suggested Tanya was here simply to cozy up to Peter."

I didn't share that she'd allegedly already *cozied up* to him at some point in time. I wasn't really sure I believed that. Or maybe I didn't want to believe it.

"Not sure how that's going to work," Seth said on a chuckle. "Our groom seems as fond of his future mother-in-law as I am of double exposures. And going after Finn didn't endear her to anyone."

I nodded, frowning. "I thought he was going to have a stroke."

Seth grinned. "He did look a bit like a boiling lobster. Hot enough to fry my camera lens."

"I'm pretty sure you prevented her imminent demise."

"I don't think Finn would have seriously done her harm."

"Don't you?" I wished I was so certain. I'd never seen such hatred in someone's eyes. It chilled me just recalling it.

"You think he might have hurt her?"

I shrugged. "I'm surprised Peter didn't intervene."

"He isn't here. He left about an hour ago with his agent."

"What?" I scanned the room as if to prove him wrong, but he wasn't. Indignation raised my hackles. "I get his celebrity mind-set of arriving late, but this isn't Hollywood. You don't show up late to a party you're hosting. And you sure as hell don't leave before your guests." *Note to self: give the actor a book on etiquette for Christmas.*

"Guess he thinks rules don't apply to him," Seth said. "Oh, say, I got a slew of great photos. I hope you'll have time to look them over before you head back to L.A. and let me know which ones you think I should suggest for their wedding album. Wow, can you believe tomorrow at this time, Meg and Peter will be married?"

His words caught me by surprise. As much as I wished nothing but the best for Meg, it hadn't really sunk in how very different our lives would be going forward. But they would be. She'd be married to a big film and TV star. I'd still be a Key Wardrobe. A single woman in L.A. I'd still be invited to parties at their house, and we'd have the occasional girls' night out, but she was going to be busy. Probably too busy for me.

No. Don't dwell on that. If you do, you won't get through tomorrow. "Sure, I'd love to go over those photos with you."

"Great."

I peered into those sexy brown eyes and swore I saw something different there, something like interest in me as more than an old pal. My heart beat a little faster. This was a sweet wrap to a sour couple of days, but it was also dangerous. *Don't fall for a guy you can't have a serious relationship with, Daryl Anne. Heartache City. Not a destination I wanted to book.*

"Seth…I…"

"Yes?" He leaned toward me and something hot curled in my lower body. Something kind of delicious.

"Er, uh, I'm heading home. I'll see you tomorrow."

He looked disappointed, but didn't push it. "Sure. Sweet dreams, Blessing."

I went to the table to get my purse, intending to let Meg know that I was leaving. But when I saw her, I stayed put. Tanya had her ear, waving her hands as she spoke in quiet undertones. Conning

Meg, I was sure. Acting like the victim. Playing her everyone-hates-me card to the only person in the room who might believe that innocent act. Meg could be a strong advocate for an underdog. That fierce loyalty was a gift. I hoped she didn't forget that she'd inherited that gift from her dad, who I noticed had also gone.

As I headed toward the door, Ash stopped me. "What's up with that woman? Meg should be bubbling over with joy and anticipation. But look at that crease between her brows. And she's nibbling on her lower lip. If this keeps up, she'll have frown lines only a Botox injection or plastic surgery can erase. We need to rescue her."

I decided Ash was right. I started to follow her toward Meg, but a blaze of color stepped into my path. Zelda had a wild glint in her eyes. I figured I was about to get an earful for not keeping Tanya away from Big Finn. Instead of flying at me like an irate parakeet, however, she caught my arm and dragged me to one side. She spoke in a voice just above a whisper. "Oh my god, Daryl Anne, there's a problem at the wedding site. I don't want to upset Meg or Peter. Will you come with me, please?"

"What sort of a problem?" And why was this my concern? She was the expert at setting up the event. I was just a lowly maid of honor.

"I'm not sure." If she truly were the little bird she appeared to be at that moment, her wings would be fluttering, her feathers puffed. She chirped, "Don't react, but the police were called."

Don't react? How did I not react to that? I gasped. "The police?"

My pulse tripped, and she looked ready to pass out. "Yes. That suggests it's really bad. Right?"

"Maybe," I said noncommittally, but I feared it might. I let her drag me out to the parking lot.

She handed me a ring of keys. "Could you drive? I'm too rattled."

Like I was any calmer?

* * *

Maybe it was the two police cars, lights flashing in the center of the Tie the Knot parking lot that brought back the queasiness in my empty stomach. *Why the show of authority?* Okay, two police cars might not seem like such a big deal where you live, but in this small town, it meant something more serious than Mrs. Dunworthy's cat getting stuck in a tree. More serious than the Bennett brothers whacking mailboxes. As serious as…as… my wanting to strangle Meg's mom.

Zelda knew it too. "Jeez, you'd think they'd found a dead body."

"What?" I gasped. *Oh, God, they hadn't, had they?*

Zelda pulled at her hair until it looked like raffia ribbons. "I can't hold a wedding with crime scene tape plastered everywhere."

The incongruity of the remark had me blinking. Sure. Forget someone might have been murdered…just focus on pulling off the wedding. As if Meg and Peter would want to exchange vows where someone had been slain. "Let's not jump to conclusions. No one said anything about homicide. Did they?"

She didn't answer. Just tugged on her hair again. "What if this brings the press? Peter will have a cow." She groaned and flopped forward, a face plant into her hands.

I glanced around. "There's no press here now. Not even Kramer."

Thank God. "Maybe we can ask the sheriff to keep whatever has occurred under wraps until after the ceremony."

Zelda shot me a get-real glare. I swallowed hard. *I'd lost my mind for a second there.* Gossip sped through this town like electricity through a wire. *Zing.* Before the ten o'clock news started, word would have spread to every household. Her fingers snatched at her hair again. "I wanted everything to be perfect for Meg."

I caught her wrist, halting the manic compulsion. "Meg might prefer that her wedding planner not end up bald."

She blanched. "I'm representing Peter and Meg. Appearance is as important as remaining cool and dealing with whatever hiccups occur." She lowered the passenger visor, made a little squawk at the image reflected in the tiny mirror, and finger-combed her hair until it lost the mad-scientist aspect. She reapplied lip gloss. Then nodded. "Okay. Let's do this."

We exited Zelda's Prius. Daylight savings time. Although evening was at least an hour away, the sky was still blue and sunny without the usual breeze that could be part of early June weather. The serenity I'd felt in this setting earlier today, however, seemed nothing but a dream. I sensed instead an air of desecration. A faint scent. A vibration. Tangible, yet indefinable. Perhaps it was only my mood given the past couple of hours, given the unsettling claims Tanya had made.

Troy and an older man that I recognized as Sheriff Gooden were interviewing the gate guard. I overheard a few snatches of conversation as we strode toward them. Nothing said seemed to have anything to do with our reason for being there. Maybe whatever had happened wasn't as bad as I'd been imagining.

"Ah, Ms. Blessing, Ms. Love," the sheriff said. "Glad you could make it so promptly."

I felt Troy's gaze drilling into me. No surprise. He was probably still pissed about our exchange earlier.

Zelda didn't even glance at the younger man. She addressed his superior, all signs of the hysteria she'd displayed in the car gone. Or hidden. "Sheriff, what's happened?"

"Well, ma'am, we're just trying to figure out how this could have happened."

"I didn't ask *how*. I asked *what*."

My nerves twitched. But Zelda began tapping her foot, impatience wafting off her like stinky perfume.

"It's a real shame, that's what it is," the gate guard said, not looking her in the eye, his gaze falling to the pavement. "A real shame."

His avoidance tactics increased my anxiety. But surely it wasn't that someone had been injured or killed. Otherwise the county police or the coroner would have arrived before us. At the least, an ambulance. I glanced from the sheriff to Troy. "Do you suppose one of you gentlemen might let us know why we're here?"

Troy scratched his neck. "Vandalism."

I frowned. "Like what? Graffiti on the church walls?"

"No, ma'am," the sheriff said without elaborating.

But I knew I'd asked the wrong question the second I asked it. The sheriff wouldn't have involved Zelda if that were something to do with either the small or large church. This had to do with Meg's wedding. I recalled the billowing tent being erected earlier, and my stomach did a slow roll. "Exactly what was vandalized?"

I again directed my question at Troy, having given up on getting a straight answer from the sheriff or the gate guard. Meg's former beau didn't look upset, but more like he was holding back a grin. An ugly suspicion sneaked through me. Had Troy been the vandal?

He said, "The chairs set up for the Reilly-Wolfe nuptials were upended. Several were smashed."

I clutched my middle as if the band of my arms could keep me from getting ill again, because a few damaged chairs were hardly worthy of the police being called out. "And…?"

"The anchor ties on the tent were cut, the tent itself slashed to ribbons."

"And all that blood," the gate guard said sounding as though he, too, might be ill.

My knees wobbled.

Zelda gasped. "Blood?"

Somehow I managed to ask, "Human blood?"

Troy shrugged. "Won't know until we run tests."

The sheriff stepped in. Finally. "Now ladies, there's no cause for you to be this upset. I'm sure a couple of phone calls, Ms. Love, and you can get this all fixed up again before the wedding tomorrow."

"A couple of phone calls? At this time of night? Everything's closed. Tomorrow's Sunday. No one will be in any office until Monday morning. Too late. Too late." Zelda's skin had turned a color six shades lighter than her Crayola-yellow hair. She staggered on her feet, looking ready for another face plant, this one into the tarmac of the parking lot.

The sheriff caught her by the upper arms. "Ms. Love, are you all right? You don't look so good."

That seemed to bring her around. Zelda muttered something that sounded like, "Never let them see you sweat." She shook her head a couple of times and inhaled deeply. Then she pulled loose of the sheriff's hold and straightened her dress. "Show me. Now."

The guard led the way. Zelda caught hold of me and pulled me along. The two cops had trouble keeping up. When we arrived, the sight was worse even than I'd pictured. Zelda made a small animal sound. Her hand flew to her chest as she took in the mess, her expression that of an insurance adjuster itemizing the damage. Her cheeks puffed in and out, then she spun toward the guard and splayed her hands in exasperation. "How could you have allowed someone in who would do this?"

"We think he came on the waterside, ma'am," the sheriff said, a bit breathless from the fast pace Zelda had set arriving at the crime scene.

"But why?" She seemed to be asking the question of the universe rather than anyone present.

Nonetheless, the guard answered, "Because the only folks I allowed in were the setup crew you hired, the wedding party, and you, Ms. Love."

"I think she wants to know why someone did this, not why we think they came by boat," Troy said. He stared at me when he spoke, as if challenging me to accuse him. Instead of stilling my suspicions of him, that raised them.

It also sent a shiver through me. Someone had been trying to ruin Meg's wedding as early as yesterday. No one had as much motive as Troy.

The sheriff said, "There's no accounting for the reasons criminals do stuff like this."

"Well, I have to get this fixed. Immediately." Zelda began digging in her purse for a cell phone, and that's when I recalled we'd left the restaurant without retrieving our phones. "Oh, no. I don't have my phone."

Zelda gazed at me as if I had an answer. "I can go back for your phone. Or have someone bring it."

"No. I don't want anyone else to know about this until I can make it right. Oh God, how am I going to find replacements this time of night?"

I had an idea. I hit Troy up for his phone and dialed, hoping Seth had retrieved his phone by now. "Hey, where'd you go?"

I avoided his question and instead asked one of my own, "Are you still at the restaurant?"

"Just about to leave. Why?"

"Could you go back inside and get my phone and Zelda's and bring them to the wedding site right now. Without telling anyone where you're going?"

"Sounds mysterious. What's up?"

"I'll explain when you get here. Thanks, Seth." I rang off.

"You'll have your phone in a couple of minutes, Zelda."

She gave me a wobbly but grateful smile. "Thank God the flowers hadn't been delivered."

The Tie the Knot events director arrived. Melvin Bates, the epitome of efficiency from ready-for-action work boots to a no-nonsense attitude, was a lean, black man with a sleek haircut and a charming manner that seemed like a ray of sunlight through a storm cloud. Obviously, this wasn't Melvin's first pre-wedding fiasco. Even better, he came prepared with possible solutions.

After offering several heartfelt apologizes, he told Zelda, "I'm thinking we could relocate the ceremony to the gazebo. It's right next to the water and very lovely this time of year."

"Oh, I just don't know. Mr. Wolfe was very insistent on a tent." Zelda's hand inched close to her hair. I shook my head at her in warning. She stayed her hand.

Melvin said, "You'd still be able to use all of your other

decorations, and it will take no time to set up tomorrow. Which, of course, our staff will do for you. And since the wedding party is small, I believe we might also have enough on-site chairs to accommodate your needs."

"Well…I suppose that could be an option. I guess you'd better show me." The color began returning to Zelda's cheeks as she grasped on to the hope being offered by the events director. The two went off to check out the gazebo and the chairs in the stockroom.

Troy and I ended up alone. After a silent, uncomfortable few moments, I said, "I should probably go back to the parking lot to wait for Seth."

As I turned away, he said, "You think I did this, don't you?"

I stiffened, but didn't answer. I glanced back at him.

Troy's eyes narrowed. "We used to be friends, Daryl Anne."

I knew I should just walk away, let this go, but my last nerve had been stomped on. I blew out an exasperated breath. "That was before you broke my best friend's heart, before you crashed her bachelorette party acting like you were the groom, before you promised to ruin her wedding."

He arched an eyebrow, holding his hands up as though surrendering. But a contrite grin tamped my anger, as did his next words, "Okay. Point taken. But I've sworn to enforce the law, not break it. I wouldn't do this."

No. He wouldn't. He'd take the bull by the horns. Go after Meg in person. Try to sweep her off her feet. Not destroy property that belonged to innocent second parties. I relented. "I'm sorry."

"Thank you." He fell into step beside me, and we walked toward the parking lot.

"Now, who do you think would do something like this?"

I shrugged. I'd thought it was one of the other wedding party, but no one had slipped out of the dinner that I was aware of. Then again, could I be sure? I had been in the bathroom a long time. "I don't know."

"Who do you think sent those pictures of Meg and me, er, dancing?"

"No idea." I suspected Tanya had sent them, and that was before I knew her motive. But after learning that she and Peter had a history, she'd leaped right to the top of my suspect list. Then again, what if Kramer had lied? What if he just wanted to hurt Tanya for ignoring him? I decided not to tell Troy anything that might get him riled up on Meg's behalf. I looked around at the mess again and felt a finger of ice along my spine. "Obviously someone, besides you, doesn't want this wedding to come off."

"What about that cameraman? He didn't seem too happy about being left out of the party last night."

"Kramer?" I recalled how pissed off he was earlier this evening and considered whether that indicated a vindictive nature. Even if it did, what motive would he have to keep Peter and Meg from marrying? "Wouldn't he take his anger out on Tanya, not Meg and Peter?"

"Yeah, probably."

"And since he wasn't there last night, he wouldn't have been able to get his hands on Meg's phone to send the photos to anyone."

"That's true." He sounded as disappointed as I felt. "Though I have to admit, I'd prefer the perp was a stranger."

And not someone we know and consider friend or family. I nodded in total agreement. "Is it ever that neat?"

"Not usually."

Zelda caught up with us, resolution in her step. A smile had smoothed away the frown lines. "Good news, guys. The ceremony won't be as private as Peter insisted upon, but given the circumstances, it will do. Nicely, in fact. As soon as Seth arrives with my phone, I'll be able to call the florist and the workers I have scheduled tomorrow to explain the slight alteration in our plans. Oh, Troy, Sheriff Gooden wants you to help him gather the tent to take in for evidence."

"Will you be checking the damaged chairs for fingerprints?" Zelda asked.

Troy shook his head. "We aren't likely to find any viable prints since none of the workers were wearing gloves today."

"So I suppose they'll just get away with it." Zelda huffed. "Unless there's surveillance video somewhere on the grounds. Is there, Troy?"

"There is, but the cameras were damaged in that bad storm we had last month and haven't been replaced yet."

"Don't tell me, Mr. Knott can't afford a new one? That man has to have more money than God."

I could see her working herself up again. I touched her arm gently. "Let's concentrate on what you can do, Zelda, and not on what you can't do anything about."

"I want whoever did this prosecuted."

"We all do. But it probably isn't going to happen," I said. "And you aren't in charge of that. Why not let Troy and the sheriff do their jobs while you do yours?"

Her sigh mimicked a tire losing air. "I suppose you're right. Oh look, here's Seth now."

My breath snagged, a thrill I didn't like sweeping the length of me. I thought I'd moved beyond my old feelings for Seth, that the crush was a teenage thing, but somehow it seemed to be growing stronger. *You're going back to Los Angeles on Monday. Get a grip.* I really needed to find a boyfriend. In L.A. This celibate thing was not working for me.

"Do you have my phone?" Zelda said, beelining for Seth. He held up two phones. She snatched hers with a joyful cry. "Thank you, thank you. I really have to get home and start making calls. Seth would you mind driving Daryl Anne?"

"Not at all," he said, handing over my cell phone. Our fingers brushed, and a warm *zing* swept up my arm and straight into my heart. *Darn it.*

"Now where did I put my keys?" Zelda began digging in her sweater and then her purse. A second later her gaze cut to me. "I believe you have my car keys, Daryl Anne."

"Oh, of course." I reached into the pocket of my dress, and as my fingers found the keys, they also encountered the envelope I'd forgotten putting there earlier in the evening. The one Kramer had given me at the dinner. I hadn't opened it or read it. I lifted it out now. My name was lettered as if a child had printed it.

Zelda took her keys and took off. "See you both tomorrow."

"See you." I felt Seth's curious gaze and met his intense stare.

"So what went on? Why are the cops here?"

I sighed. As we walked to his car, I brought him up to speed.

"First those incriminating photos and now this...?"

I tapped the unopened envelope against my palm absently.

Seth eyed the envelope curiously. "What's that?"

I shrugged. "Someone left it for me at the dinner tonight. With everything else going on I completely forgot about it."

I tore it open. The cover of the card had a bride and groom

holding champagne glasses, toasting each other. I frowned. It wasn't a thank-you note. More like a card for a shower gift. Inside was more hand-lettered printing. My skin broke out in goose bumps.

If you don't stop this wedding, I will.

Chapter 10

The day of the wedding

*H*appy is the bride the sun shines on...

The morning dawned with clear skies, breathless air, and a kiss of warmth. As perfect as a day in late July. I doubted Meg would be happy though when she found out Troy was attending the ceremony. In his official capacity.

Seth insisted we show the threatening note to the police. Sheriff Gooden insisted Troy be present to keep anyone from following through on the threat. I wasn't positive that Troy wouldn't disrupt the wedding, but he hadn't seem pleased about being ordered to make sure no one else did.

I shuffled into the kitchen, my eyes puffy from lack of sleep, my mind spinning with everything I needed to get done today. There were too many worrisome, unknown elements at play. The aroma of coffee pulled me into the kitchen. I expected to find Mom and Billie chatting over their favorite brew, but only Gram sat at the breakfast bar, newspaper spread out, as she read the morning edition while eating poached eggs.

She glanced up as I drew near, her good morning smile shifting into a raised-brow grimace. "Looks like you've been on a two-day drunk. You might want to put some of those cucumbers I bought the other day on those eyes, Daryl Anne."

"I had two glasses of wine. Two. My max." I filled a mug with coffee. "Where's Mom?"

"Still in bed."

She'd had a late night. Very late. But that was so unlike her that I couldn't imagine where she'd gone or what she'd been doing. "Her car wasn't here when I got home. I wanted to talk to her. I waited up, but I didn't hear her come in."

Gram sighed, the sound feeling like a brick dropped onto the breakfast bar. "I have to tell you, I haven't seen Susan that upset since…well, since your daddy died. And before you ask, she wouldn't tell me why. All I know is that awful woman did something to rile her up."

I sipped the steaming coffee, afraid to glance at Gram. She could read my giveaway expression as if it were a bold-print ad in *The Weddingville Weekly*. "No one needs to worry about it much longer," I said. "I'm sure Tanya isn't sticking around after the wedding today."

"Thank the good lord."

But what would stick around was the fallout from her accusations about my father. As much as I wanted answers, I didn't want them from Gram. I wasn't sure she could take the stress, and I wasn't sure it was wise to add to the mental burdens already weighing on me today. And yet, as I drank my coffee, a part of me waited for Mom to wake up and join us.

All right, I admit it. I dreaded opening a Pandora's box that I might afterward wish I'd left shut. But the lock had been pried off. I'd been allowed a peek inside, and I wasn't sure

I'd ever be satisfied not knowing for sure. *Even if it breaks your heart?*

After half hour and some dry toast to soak up the acid in my stomach, I gave up on my mother. I sliced a couple of cucumbers and headed to the shower. On days like this, with my schedule packed and spare time at a premium, I adored short, no-fuss hair. I set my brush aside. Meg and Ash would add the finishing touches to my makeup and that of her bridesmaids later on so I didn't bother with more than some eyeliner and mascara. The cucumbers had reduced the swelling and redness. *Thank goodness.* I tossed on some sweats and realized I needed to do a load of laundry before packing tomorrow.

I opened the lid to the washer and tossed stuff in. One sock leaped out and landed in the wastebasket. As I reached to retrieve it, I spied a flash of color beneath it. Frowning, I lifted the wad of fabric from the basket, realizing as it unfolded that it was the fuchsia dress my mother had worn to the dinner last night. The hair on my nape twitched. What the hell? Mom had to have been really upset to toss the dress away. It was new. And she'd looked beautiful in it. On the other hand, maybe she never wanted to see it again because it would always remind her of the nasty encounter with Tanya.

As I stared at the floral pattern, I recalled every moment of that awful scene in the restaurant's ladies' room. My hand began to shake. I blinked, swallowed a throat full of disgust, and fought to rein in my temper. My gaze narrowed on the dress. The urge to rip it to shreds swept through me, a repulsive impulse that went against the very core of my upbringing. I created garments and mended whenever possible, always with an eye toward preservation. Not destruction.

This dress, I realized, already had a large tear near the right shoulder and the matching belt was missing. Mom had obviously had the same reaction as me. Only she'd acted on it. Another indicator of her unusual distress. I started to ball up the dress, but froze when my fingers brushed something like dried mud or rust near the hem. A lot of it. Splatters not just at the hem, but across the skirt. My throat wanted to close. Just where had Mom gone after dropping Billie off at home last night? What had she done? How did this—whatever it was—get all over her dress?

The doorbell rang. I jumped like a guilty kid. But I hadn't done anything wrong. I hadn't worn this dress. Hadn't caused the splatters. The rip. A nervous laugh escaped from me. I stuffed the dress back into the basket. Mom and I would be discussing this later today or tonight whether she wanted to or not.

The bell sounded again. Meg and the bridesmaids were dressing here. Gram had gone down to get the shop set up for the scheduled customers and walk-ins. Mom's room was empty too, I saw. She must have risen while I was showering. I doubted either would answer the back door. I hurried to the elevator, shoving the puzzle of the soiled dress from my mind. I owed Meg my focus. This was her day.

We were to be delivered by town cars to Tie the Knot. Meg would be riding with her father. I felt a pang of envy. Not that I wished I was getting married, but that my dad could be here to walk me down the aisle when I did finally wed. But thoughts of my dad today only brought to mind Tanya. I wasn't going there. Not now anyway.

I wrenched the door open, fake smile plastered on. To my surprise, only Meg stood there. "Meg! You must be excited. You're early."

Her cheeks were flushed, indicating her emotions were running high. I hoped it was a happy high, even as I realized something was amiss. I tugged her inside and into the elevator to the top floor. "What's going on?"

She didn't say a word, just led me into the kitchen and helped herself to some coffee. Worry scurried through me. A quiet Meg equaled trouble. She must have heard about the switch in venues. About the vandalism. About Troy? I couldn't stand the silence, but wanted to reassure her. "Zelda has it—"

"You were right." She cut me off, lifting her chin like someone determined not to cry. No matter what. Why did being right make my stomach ache? My mind ran the gambit of things she could be referring to. Right about Peter being a diva? Right about her not marrying a man if she wasn't one-hundred-percent sure she loved him? And only him? Right about her still having feelings for Troy?

I ran my tongue over my dry lips as I leaned across the breakfast bar, studying her. "I'm sorry, Meg, but I'm going to need more clues to figure out what you're talking about."

"My mother."

Okay... this I didn't expect. I scrambled trying to recall everything I'd ever said about Tanya. Too much to pin down to any one item. "I'm not sure whether to apologize or—"

"I shouldn't have invited her." A blush crept up her neck.

I clamped my mouth shut, sensing that I shouldn't interrupt.

Meg swallowed. "Or reconnected with her. Or had anything to do with her. Ever. She doesn't really care about me. She never did."

I braced for the flood of tears, empathy washing through me. But no tears came. Meg's eyes remained as cool as jade. The oddity of this struck sheer terror across my heart. I'd never seen my chaotic friend so seriously calm and resigned. Well, at least, not since that long-ago day when she'd told me that her mother was never coming back. I reached across the breakfast bar and touched her hand. "Oh, Meg, I'm so sorry."

"No. Don't be. I can't deal with sympathy right now. I'd fall apart, and I'll be damned if she's going to ruin my wedding."

At that moment, I wanted to find Tanya Reilly Jones and plant her six feet under. I stifled my fury. If I lost it, Meg would suffer more. But damn, I couldn't stand to see her like this. I blinked back my own tears. The last thing she needed or wanted was me falling apart on her behalf. But oh, the helpless feeling. "You want me to hunt her down and shoot her? 'Cause I'd willingly go to jail for you."

Meg smirked and shook her head. "Thank you. But no. Besides, she's gone. Left town. Without so much as a good-bye."

Why did that surprise me? I suppose because, when I'd left the restaurant last night, they'd been thick as thieves. Or so it seemed. I mean Tanya had Meg's full attention, laying it on as thick as peanut butter. I sighed. *Conning her,* I'd thought at the time. Looked like I was right, whether or I liked it or not. "Meg, I..."

But what could I say? Nothing that would ease the pain she had to be feeling.

"It's all right, Daryl Anne. I fantasized some crazy expectations. That's what comes of living in La La Land, I guess. I started to believe in happy endings. Fool. Stupid, dumb fool."

I hated that she was berating herself. That the most important female in her life was such a disappointment and worse.

"I can't believe she didn't say good-bye..." I said, thinking out loud. "She was doing an article on Weddingville. Surely she wouldn't take off without notifying someone. In a text? Or an e-mail?"

"Actually, she sent a text. It said: 'Something came up. Sorry.'"

Cold. Like the woman herself. No heart. No feelings for anyone except herself. I was a fool too, for thinking I'd seen some flashes of vulnerability and humanity in Tanya. At the time, I told myself even the worst of us usually has some sort of soft spot. Only how much humanity had she shown my mother? And to abandon Meg twice? My hands tightened around my coffee mug. If I ever crossed paths with Tanya again, I'd give her a soft spot.

I kept these thoughts to myself, hoping Meg wouldn't read my face and know.

She sighed. "I'd like to get ready for my wedding and not think about anything else today."

"Then you came to the right place," I said in my best-friend-has-your-back voice. "Are you sure you'll be able to get through the ceremony?"

"Yes. I have you and Dad and Peter and that's all I need."

"You do. We'll make this the most wonderful wedding ever."

"Damn straight." She gave a toss of her fiery hair and glanced toward the window. Sunlight glinted off the green water. Seagulls dipped and soared. "It's so nice outside. I'm sorry the ceremony is taking place under that tent."

I blanched. Oh, no. She hadn't heard. Why hadn't Zelda let her know? Did Peter know yet?

"Daryl Anne, your eyebrows are dancing like marionettes. What's the matter?"

"Er, ah, I'm surprised that Zelda didn't tell you."

"Probably couldn't reach me. I misplaced my phone again."

I rolled my eyes. "Let's hope it doesn't get you in as much trouble as it did last time."

She laughed. "I need to put it on a chain around my neck."

"Exactly."

"Zelda should be overseeing the final details at the venue right now. Has a problem come up?"

"Not today." Not that I knew of anyway. "But last night…" As gently as possible, I explained what had happened to the tent and the switch to the gazebo, omitting the threatening note and Sheriff Gooden's insistence that Troy oversee the ceremony.

Meg's green eyes widened, and the first sign of delight shone in their depths. "Really? I don't know whether to be angry or distressed or thankful."

I frowned, growing more confused. I'd expected her to be swearing and vowing to throttle whoever had tried to ruin things. "Why thankful?"

"The gazebo was my first choice. Peter wanted the tent, in case any paparazzi showed up or flew over in helicopters. I think he thinks he's a bigger celebrity than he is." Meg stretched like a lazy cat.

I bit back a full-on grin. I thought he was a bigger celebrity than she realized and feared when she discovered that it might be too much for her to handle. "Well, it's going to be so gorgeous."

"Everything I ever dreamed."

"Except for your mother being there." The words slipped out before I could stop them.

"Well, you can't have everything," she said, pressing her lips together. I had the distinct impression that she thought that, if she told herself that, she'd wouldn't be sad.

My heart cried for my best friend, but I put on the biggest smile I owned and hugged her. "Come on. We can't go to a wedding looking like this. There's makeup to apply and hair to fix. Gowns to be donned."

"Ash should be here any moment to get things started."

* * *

The bridesmaids arrived, smiling and laughing and rallying around Meg, lifting her spirits. Ash Moon showed up last, bringing all the hair supplies and makeup. And Meg's wayward phone.

"Peter has been texting and phoning," Ash said, handing the cell to its owner.

Meg took the phone, then sighed. "I can't remember my password. I lose the phone so often, I am paranoid about it. What did I change it to this week?"

"Your wedding day date, remember?" Ash laughed. "I keep mine the same so that I never forget. My favorite day of the year—twelve twenty-five. Christmas."

"You'll both have to change passwords now that we all know the current ones," Jade said.

"No way," Ash said. "Then I wouldn't remember mine."

Meg was reading the texts Ash told her about, a frown creasing her smooth forehead. She glanced at me, worry radiating from her. "Oh, dear. Peter found out about the change in venue, and he's breathing fire."

My stomach did a little roll. If he was upset about no tent, imagine what he'd do when he discovered that Troy would be attending in his official capacity. "Nothing to be done about it, unless he wants to postpone the ceremony."

Meg's eyes rounded at the suggestion. "Don't even think that. This wedding is taking place today. In Weddingville. And if he can't deal with that, then I guess he can just marry someone else."

Spoken like a bride-to-be who is sure of her man. And yet, I had the oddest sensation that she would live to regret those words even as her fingers flew across the virtual keyboard of her smartphone.

"Let's get this party started," Ash said, waving a thick makeup brush.

Meg perked up. Hair and makeup were her world. She could disappear into the creativity and put her troubles on hold. She let herself be swept into the circle of female chatter and laughter, more raucous than anyone. No one would suspect her inner turmoil.

Ash was hired by the studio fresh out of beauty school. She'd been a quick study, learning everything Meg could teach her and coming up with a few innovations of her own. She transformed the whole lot of us from everyday into head-turners. Seth arrived as she was finishing up with Meg. He wore another white dress shirt and chinos with pockets for film. I knew he preferred film to digital for wedding photos.

His familiar scent wound into me like a velvet hook, digging into my heart, tugging my emotions. I fought the pull. But when he went all shy-guy in front of the giddy bridesmaids, I lost my grip. I was falling hard for this guy. Damn. I didn't want to. My life was in California. I'd get over this crush-gone-viral. That's what I'd do. Somehow.

Ash interrupted my romantic musings. "There you go."

She moved aside, giving us a view of Meg. My mouth dropped open. Seth's camera clicked.

"Meg, you're breathtaking," someone said. I couldn't be sure who. My gaze was fixed on my best friend. Her flame-red hair tumbled around her face in curls, kissing her bare shoulders, giving her skin a peaches-and-cream hue and making her eyes look like giant, sparkling emeralds.

Even she was impressed. "Wow, Ash. I'm going to have to give you a raise."

"Hey," Ash beamed, "you all heard that. You're my witnesses."

Everyone laughed.

Seth said, "And I got it on film."

Meg blushed.

Seth took several candid shots and a few group photos, then we chased him out of the apartment until we'd all donned our gowns. We descended to the second level, to an area of the shop that Gram and Mom had set up to resemble a church interior. There Seth had us pose for more formal photos, several with Meg holding her bouquet, a couple with her showing off the garter. The energy among the group was joyous.

Billie interrupted us, sweeping into the room with Big Finn in her wake. He presented a surprisingly dashing figure in his three-piece tuxedo. He'd slicked his shock of red hair into place. He gaze went straight to his daughter, and he gasped. Tears glistened in his eyes. "No bride was ever so beautiful."

Meg shuddered and smiled weakly. "Don't make me cry, Dad. It'll ruin my makeup."

He nodded, sucked in a breath, and withdrew an oblong jewelry box from an inner jacket pocket. "It's a good thing, then, that I'm not wearing makeup."

My heart hitched.

Before the room broke into a collective weep-fest, Gram said, "Your dad and I wanted to make sure that you have your something old, something new, something borrowed, something blue, Meg."

Mom slipped silently into the room. Ours gazes met, and she looked away. Just as well. This wasn't our moment. It was Meg's.

"I have a blue garter," Meg said, flashing her leg again. "And my shoes and gown are new."

"Well, then, this would qualify as something old," Big Finn

said, opening the jewelry box to reveal a single strand of peach-colored pearls with a diamond clasp. "These belonged to your great-grandmother Reilly. She wore them for her wedding and passed them to her daughter, my mother, when she married my father. Now they're yours, Meg."

Meg gingerly lifted the necklace from the box, her eyes glazed with unshed tears, and for a second, I thought Ash was going to have to redo her makeup. "Oh, Dad, this is so perfect."

She turned her back to him, carefully lifting her hair so that he could hook the clasp. She spun toward the mirror and sighed. "So perfect."

"Ah, but that still leaves something borrowed," Billie said, stepping forward. She produced a small velvet box of her own. "These diamond stud earrings were a gift from my late husband on our twenty-fifth wedding anniversary. Fool man. I don't even have pierced ears. I've never worn them, but I treasure them, and I'd be honored if you'd wear them on your special day, Meg."

"Oh, Billie, thank you so much. Darn, you're all conspiring to ruin my makeup." Her smile wobbled, and Ash daubed the dampness near her eyes without smearing the mascara. Seth caught the special, once-in-a-lifetime moments on film.

"Hey, look at the time," Meg cried suddenly. "If we don't leave now, I'll be late for my wedding."

"I'll get you there on time, baby, don't you worry." Big Finn offered his arm, and his smiling daughter gladly accepted, her mood seeming as light as a balloon.

I just wished my heavy sense of impending disaster would fill with air and float away.

Chapter 11

The Wedding

The day seemed to have a life of its own, a pulse as primitive as the incoming tide lapping at the shore. A force of nature. Persistent. Persevering. Unstoppable. I stole to a door and slipped outside, anxious to ensure that nothing was amiss. Despite the clear sky and warm sun, gooseflesh broke across my exposed arms and shoulders, chilling me.

Arriving guests found seats on the padded folding chairs that faced the gazebo, their voices muted in deference to the trio of musicians playing Muzak. I rubbed my arms as I stood in the shadows. Watching. The bridesmaids, Meg, Big Finn, and I had been ushered into a private area off the ballroom to wait until the ceremony commenced. But I was too fidgety to stay put. I had the same butterflies in my stomach I got every time our sitcom filmed before a live audience. I would stand backstage, eyeing the costumes one last time, checking the set, counting the audience members.

I scanned the guests, who all seemed appropriately dressed

for "small town wedding." Not that I cared what anyone was wearing—unless it was meant to disrupt the ceremony. I spotted nothing to set off my danger meter, and yet it beeped like a smoke alarm needing a fresh battery. *Think about something else, Daryl Anne. Be present in the now. Enjoy.* I shifted my gaze to the surroundings, and as I took in the beauty before me, a sweet sensation of delight eclipsed my worry. *If I ever get married, I'm hiring Zelda Love as my wedding planner.*

Golden ribbons stretched between the rows of padded chairs, anchored at each gap with a stand of creamy roses, blocking guests from using the white runner to access the seating. The rug, like a path of white sand leading to the gazebo, was sprinkled with peach-hued rose petals. Just beyond, at the edge of the shore, the huge, filigreed gazebo was bedecked in ribbons and roses, sparkling as if sprinkled with fairy dust.

Beautiful. Nothing out of place. Why did that worry me?

"What are you doing out here?"

I started. Troy. Dressed in a suit less formal than the groomsmen, he stood out in a crowd of good-looking men.

"I…I…" I avoided his gaze, not wanting him to know I didn't fully trust his intentions today. But when had I become a coward? I lifted my head, meeting his bright blue eyes. "Can you blame me, after last night, for being anxious?"

"No need. Nothing out of the norm so far."

So far. That was what worried me. "Are you the only police officer present?"

He shook his head, glancing away as though we weren't discussing anything more serious than the balmy weather. "There are a couple of others, disguised as guests."

He swung his gaze back to me. "Is Meg in there?"

Where else would she be? "Why?"

"I want to see her."

"No." I didn't trust his motives farther than the sea is from the shore. "No."

"Just for a minute."

"It's not a good idea."

"Why not?"

Did I have to spell it out for him? "You're only here to keep an eye out for the person making the threats."

"Are you afraid if Meg talks to me that she'll call off the wedding?"

"No." But I couldn't be sure of it. As I turned to leave, I spied Ash eyeing Troy as if he were a problem she needed to solve for Meg's sake. Hoping she didn't act on the impulse, I slipped inside, shutting the door.

Meg grasped my hand, startling me, whispering loud enough to wake the dead, "What is Troy doing here?"

The heat drained from my face, and I couldn't swallow over the punch bowl-size lump in my throat. She was minutes away from walking down that white aisle to stand at that sparkling gazebo and exchange vows with Peter. If I told her about the threatening note, it would make her more anxious than I was. And I didn't know for sure if it was a real threat. Oh, who was I kidding? Someone has slashed the tent to ribbons, splashed blood on it. Of course, the threat was genuine.

"Daryl Anne Blessing, what aren't you telling me? Why is Troy at my wedding?"

"I guess he couldn't stay away." It wasn't a lie exactly. After all, he had been ordered to be here.

She bit her lower lip. "Troy better not say or do anything to upset Peter."

There wasn't as much conviction in her voice as I'd liked to have heard. I feared she was going to go ahead with this wedding, no matter what, even if she had a heart full of doubts. I wanted to tell her again that, if she had misgivings, it wasn't too late. *Sometimes the bravest thing is to back out of a marriage before you get into it. Even if it's minutes before exchanging vows.* But Meg seemed determined to see this through. She already knew how I felt. This was her life, not mine. I opted to butt out, hoping I wouldn't live to regret that.

We returned to the waiting area where Big Finn was entertaining the bridesmaids with tall tales of a misspent youth. Seth had slipped into the room and was taking candid shots. He turned his lens on me, and my insides quivered sweetly. He lowered the camera, his gaze as warm as a touch on my face. "It's almost time," he informed us.

And as if on cue, Zelda bustled in, a daffodil in matching heels and a Jacqueline Kennedy pillbox hat.

Her hand went to her chest as she caught sight of Finn. Then Meg. "Oh my, you're the most lovely bride, Meg."

Meg blushed and thanked her. But a ruckus at the door drove a spike into my nerves. Big Finn went to find out the cause, gesturing that we should all step back, out of harm's way. I caught Meg and tugged her behind me. *Sure. That's me. Woman of Steel. Faster than a speeding bullet.* The thought made me sick.

But then I recognized Peter's voice. And Seth telling Big Finn, "Peter wants the main photos of the wedding party taken before the ceremony. Seems he's worried about missing the honeymoon flight."

"No," Big Finn boomed. "You're not seeing the bride before the wedding. Bad luck."

Peter swore, cajoled, pleaded. Finn wasn't backing down.

"That might be the way they do things in Hollywood, but it's not how we do them in Weddingville."

Although I couldn't hear what Seth was saying, I guessed he was trying to reason with the groom. Eventually, Peter seemed to realize that this was taking up precious moments he'd need after the ceremony. And maybe he also understood that he wouldn't win in a fight with his future father-in-law. That alpha dog had just lifted his leg and pissed all over any such notion.

Zelda stepped in and told Seth to take Peter and his grooms-men to the gazebo. Then she waited a few beats and got the rest of us moving toward the door, making sure that we all knew what we were supposed to do, where to stand. Next thing, she was guiding us outside and toward the white carpet.

As I stepped outside, my gaze took in the gathered well-wishers, smiles on their faces as they turned to watch the wedding party glide across the white carpet. Meg's voice echoed through my mind. "Perfect."

The uneasy feeling swept me again, a whispery breeze down my spine. The hairs on my nape twitched. My mouth dried. I scanned the guests, the catering staff, and the trio of musicians. Nothing I could pinpoint, but the clawing in my stomach seemed to increase with every step toward the altar.

Peter and his agent were on one side of the minister, the brides-maids on the other. Reverend Bell was white-knuckling a small black Bible as he rocked back and forth on his heels. He had the beanpole lankiness of a lifelong drinker, though I'd never known him to imbibe in anything stronger than iced tea. The virgin kind. As I took my place, the wedding march began.

All heads turned toward the end of the aisle. To Meg and Big Finn. I heard the soft click of Seth's camera somewhere behind me, then he kneeled in front of me to capture father and daughter marching toward him. *Click. Click. Click. Click.* As he rose, he winked at me. I supposed he thought to calm me, but those chocolate eyes only made my insides melt.

As Meg arrived, I saw Troy take a stand at the end of the aisle. I prayed he wouldn't disrupt the ceremony, but given the upheaval in the world, God might have more important things to do than controlling a spurned lover. Troy seemed to have forgotten why he was here. His watchful gaze had only one target. Meg. She must have sensed it. She glanced over her shoulder, then quickly turned back toward Peter. I wanted to shout at Troy to do his job.

"Dearly beloved," the minister began. I forced myself to be in the moment, though I was too anxious to enjoy it. Reverend Bell seemed to reach the if-anyone-here-knows-any-reason-why-these-two-should-not-be-joined-in-holy-wedlock-speak-now-or-forever-hold-your-peace part of the vows quicker than I'd anticipated. I held my breath. Expecting Troy to shout out his love. I was even more afraid I'd blurt out that Meg was making a mistake. Gulls cried overhead. The surf lapped the shore. But no one spoke. *Thank you.* Tension flowed out of me on an exhaled breath.

"Who gives this woman to be wed to this man?" Reverend Bell asked, his voice slurred. My attention shifted to him, and I frowned. His pupils were the pinpoints of someone high on drugs. I'd never known him to drink, but I hadn't considered drugs.

The minister started again, his words less pronounced, "Who gives this-s wo-oman…"

I glanced away, toward the water. A flash of red on the shore caught my eye. A lump about the size of an adult seal. I squinted against the glare, focusing on it.

Big Finn said, "I give—"

A collective gasp sounded behind me. I shifted around in time to see Peter catching Reverend Bell as he toppled from the gazebo headfirst. "Shit," Peter swore, grunting as he lowered the collapsed minister to the steps.

"What the hell?" Big Finn asked.

People rushed forward. Instinctively, I retreated several steps, my heart thundering in my chest.

Peter shouted, "Someone get a doctor!"

Seth held his hands wide, a human barricade, keeping the gawkers back. "People, give the man some air."

I moved out of the way too, rethinking my conclusion that the reverend might be on drugs. Perhaps he'd suffered a heart attack or stroke. The ground beneath my heel gave. I froze, glancing over my shoulder. Dear God, I'd almost stepped off the edge of the shoreline. The flash of red caught my eye again. I blinked several times, certain I must be hallucinating. Oh God. No. I wasn't. Shock speared me. My mouth opened. No sound came out. One second I couldn't breathe, the next a blood curdling scream ripped from my throat.

"Jesus. Now what?" Big Finn demanded, rushing to my side, but he froze as he took in the cause of my shrieks. Meg slipped up next to her dad. She saw it too. A body. A woman with blond hair wearing a red dress. I couldn't seem to stop screaming. Meg—usually the hysterical one—covered her mouth, her eyes bugging out. Her face turned ashen. She crumbled in a heap of crinoline and lace. Out cold.

Peter arrived and skidded to a stop. His gaze grew wide, and he made a strangling sound. He gagged, once, twice, and threw up. On Meg. The rest was a blur. I vaguely recalled Seth catching me before I too collapsed. The moment he took hold of me, his soft voice cutting through my terror, I felt the panic subsiding, as if I'd found a safe haven. He hauled me to the nearest vacant seat, and I let him wrap me in his jacket and hold me against his strong chest.

Troy shouted, "Get back. Everyone. Stand back now. This is official police business." He headed toward the body, but his first concern was Meg. He ordered Big Finn to get her away from the beach to somewhere warm. Once she was safely in her father's arms, Troy hurried to the body, speaking into his phone. No doubt ordering backup and the coroner. A siren could be heard over the din. The ambulance for Reverend Bell. EMTs flashed past me, rushing to the minister.

Even with Seth's jacket around my shoulders and him sharing his body heat, I couldn't stop shaking. "Is Reverend Bell…?"

I couldn't bring myself to ask out loud if he was dead too. A wave of nausea swept over me. *If you don't stop this wedding, I will.* I expected something, but not this. Not a dead body. I'd been underplaying the seriousness of the threat.

"I'm not sure," Seth said. "He was still breathing, but rather shallowly." We watched the EMTs strap him to a gurney and hustle him to the ambulance. "Someone said heart attack, but that might just be speculation."

Neither of us mentioned the body in the red dress. I figured Seth was afraid I'd start screaming again. I might. Just thinking about it made my skin crawl.

"Come on, Daryl Anne." Seth helped me to my feet, cradling my elbow, his other arm around my shoulder. "Let's get you inside."

Meg had revived. The beautiful bride of earlier was now a zombie in a soiled wedding gown, smeared makeup, and light-socket hair. Her eyes were dull, dazed. "Who is it?" She asked as Seth guided me into the room. "Who?"

I shook my head. I didn't know. Not for sure. But that red dress looked like the one Tanya had been wearing the night before. Tanya with the blond hair. Maybe she hadn't left town after all.

* * *

Sheriff Gooden broke the news, confirming our worst fears. Troy reassured Meg that he'd do everything possible to find out what had happened. Meg nodded, but seemed to withdraw into herself, a strange hollowness claiming her eyes, as if she'd disappeared into a place none of us could reach. Peter gave up trying in the first few seconds. He and Walter huddled, bouncing ideas of how to put a positive spin on the wedding fiasco and shocking death of his future mother-in-law.

That snapped the shock right out of me. I shrugged off Seth's jacket, cut into the conversation, and caught Peter by the lapel of his tuxedo. "What do you think you're doing?"

He tried to wrench free of my grasp, but my finger had snagged in a buttonhole, and I hung on tight. He peered down his nose and said, "Have you lost your mind?"

"Have you lost yours? Your fiancée's mother is in a body bag on her way to the morgue. Meg needs you. She should be the only thing you're thinking of right now. Not media coverage. Let your agent call your publicist. They can write a statement for the press. You. Go. Be. With. Meg."

Peter's face paled beneath his tan as he realized the room had gone quiet. Everyone was staring at us. Including Meg. Her gaze was riveted on Peter. We were all waiting for his response. I wished I could believe the contrition that softened his stance and filled his eyes. But he was too skilled an actor. I no longer trusted him to have a genuine emotion.

Peter swallowed as if ashamed of his thoughtless attitude, an Emmy-winning performance. *Someone hand him the gold statue now.* "Walter," he said to his agent, "give Simon a call. Explain the situation and have him prepare a statement to use as soon as it becomes necessary. I need to get Meg away from here."

He held his hand toward Meg and went to her side, taking her into his arms. She collapsed against him and began to sob. My fury at her insensitive fiancé dissipated. A fissure cracked across my heart, spilling a sense of helplessness through me.

At the door, Sheriff Gooden stopped them. "Don't leave town. That goes for all of you," he said to the bridal party. "I have a lot of questions that need answering. I'll be in touch as quickly as possible so as not to delay travel plans some of you likely have."

"We'll be at a hotel in Tacoma then," Peter said. "My agent will phone you the details once we've secured a reservation."

"Nope." Sheriff Gooden shook his head. "Stay in Weddingville."

Peter's protestations fell on deaf ears. I knew he was worried that word about this whole mess would bring a slew of reporters. The sheriff didn't want to hear it. Not his problem. "I said I'd get to you quickly, and I will."

I wished Seth was still beside me, but he'd been commandeered to photograph the crime scene. Crime was relatively nonexistent in this town, but whenever one was committed, the police called Seth to do the photos. It might be his first dead body. I didn't know. I hugged myself, forcing my mind away from the corpse and back to the sheriff's intention of questioning everyone. I supposed he needed to figure out how Tanya came to be in the water.

But somehow the "don't leave town" demand seemed a little too criminal-detective show for an accidental death. Did the sheriff suspect foul play?

* * *

As Seth escorted me back to Blessing's Bridal, I was swept with a sense of the surreal. Normal seemed out of place. Off-kilter after the past two hours. Customers strolling the sidewalks, enjoying the warm weather, window shopping, laughing, chatting. Traffic moved at a crawl down Front Street. Lovers held hands, grinning at each other. Mothers and daughters argued about the cost of invitations. Or flowers.

I stepped inside the bridal shop, opting for the front entrance, hoping the scents and aura would return my solid foundation. It didn't. Mom and Gram each had a different set of customers. The entourage of Mom's group oohed and ahhed over the displayed gowns. Offering conflicting opinions. Unaware of the cloud of confusion forming in the bride-to-be's eyes.

The future mother-in-law of Gram's group had ambushed the appointment, complaining the dress the bride-to-be seemed to love made her hips look fat. I wanted to shout at them all to just shut up. To be happy for this coming wedding, to support the future marriage of their friend or loved one. That life was too short. That so many things could go wrong.

Seth urged me on through the salon and the storeroom to the offices. "You want me to come up with you?"

"No. Thank you." I handed his jacket over. "For everything. I'm going to have a big glass of wine and a long bath. I just can't seem to get warm."

"Probably the shock. You might want to do some Jack Daniel's instead of wine. I hear it helps. And eat something sweet."

The idea turned my stomach. I let him out the back door. Soon after, I stepped into a bath filled with bubbles, a tumbler of whiskey at hand. The chills left after a while and I retreated to my room for a nap. When I awoke, hours later, I heard the murmur of voices in the kitchen, along with the fragrant scent of cooked food. I assumed Mom and Gram had heard the news by now and were likely anxious to get firsthand details from me, but I wasn't up for talking to anyone. Or for eating. Someone opened my door, and I feigned sleep.

I finally got up hours after the apartment grew silent. My suitcase rested on the footstool where I'd left it, partially packed. I'd forgotten my clothes in the dryer. I crept into the laundry room. As I was opening the dryer, I remembered Mom's torn dress, the splatters on the skirt, and I wondered again where she'd been last night and how the dress had ended up in that condition. I glanced into the wastebasket. The debris that had been there earlier—dryer lint and used fabric dryer sheets was still there. The dress, however, was gone.

Chapter 12

The day after the wedding

Gram had brewed a pot of coffee, and the rich aroma lured me to the kitchen. But I had the place to myself. Mom's door was still shut, but Billie's stood open. She was already awake and working in the shop. That meant I would finally have Mom to myself this morning. When she got up. No more freezing me out. She was going to answer my questions. Not sidestep the truth. I poured a cup and settled at the breakfast bar, my gaze landing on an abandoned copy of *The Weddingville Weekly*.

I flipped to the front page, noting that it was a special edition. Printed yesterday. The paper usually released on Wednesdays. Today was Monday. As I brought my mug up for a sip, the headline grabbed me. My hand froze. The mug wobbled, sloshing hot java over my fingers and onto the counter. *Murder Victim Disrupts Ceremony.*

I lowered the mug and leaned in as if getting closer to the newsprint would make the words less horrendous. As if murder could be anything but horrific. *Murder.* A shiver tracked my spine. Denial swept me. An autopsy couldn't possibly have been performed already. This was probably conjecture. Gossip. I mean, hadn't I been warned most of my life not to believe everything I read in the papers or hear on TV? Reporters made things up all the time. I lived in Los Angeles, worked in the industry, and had firsthand knowledge of how the media twisted something innocent into a salacious, attention-grabbing news item. Surely that's what this was.

I took a long swallow of coffee, needing the caffeine to clear my head. It started working immediately. Did I really think that Mr. Early, the editor of our local paper, would be so careless about a story in his precious *Weekly*? Not likely. Billie always complained about his penchant for accuracy. "That man won't accept an ad for the bridal shop unless he checks every detail with me ten times over." No. The news story, sketchy as it was, had to be true. Someone had killed Tanya.

I don't know how long I sat there, frowning. Lost in thought. Trying to figure out who and why. Motive, means, and opportunity. The motive list would be the longest. Even Mom and I had that. But who also had means? Opportunity? A thread of frustration stitched through me. Not knowing when or how Tanya had been killed limited my deductive powers. After all, shooting someone was likely easier than, say, strangling them. One allowed for distance, while the other required close contact, strength, and a garrote. Like a belt? I swallowed hard. Poisoning would be fairly easy. But stabbing not as much, and it would be messy, bloody.

My mind went to the splatters on Mom's dress. The now-missing dress. Had those stains been blood spatter? I felt ill. My mother was not a violent person. She wouldn't stab or strangle anyone, but I couldn't stop thinking about that damned dress.

Why throw it away and leave the rest of the trash in the basket? The possibilities had my skin crawling. I wasn't sure I could cope with the answer. I wanted to get on a plane and fly back to Los Angeles and bury my head in the sand. Or at least in work.

Unfortunately, the sheriff wasn't about to let me or anyone else skip out on him.

That settled it. I had to find out how Tanya died. And when. But how was I going to do that? I supposed I could call Troy, but I doubted he'd tell me anything about an ongoing murder investigation. The police had probably given Meg the details, but I couldn't, wouldn't ask her. And I wasn't Peter's favorite person at the moment. I drank some coffee as I considered and discarded options. Then I had a thought. Seth. He'd taken photos of the corpse. He could answer my question.

I got dressed. Mom's door was still closed when I emerged from my room, ready to leave. Figuring someone should know where I was going, I hunted Billie down and found her in alterations. The work area always reminded me of a seaside cottage, the carpet as blue as a tropical sea, the walls a soft gray-washed paneling with trim the color of whitecaps. Violin music whispered through the air. Gram's velour armchair had seen better days, its fabric punctured from years of use as a giant pincushion. Her feet rested on a footstool. She faced the windows that overlooked the sound, but her head was bent to her hand-stitching. The buyer of the Vera Wang gown wanted extra bling attached to the bodice.

"Good morning," I said, bending to kiss her cheek, grateful that at least one area of my life remained familiar. Steadfast. Billie had finally decided to believe what her doctor kept telling her. Her wrist was healed. Doing what she excelled at would work out the lingering stiffness.

"Are you okay?" she asked, avoiding the more obvious questions. But we both knew she was referring to the wedding fiasco and Tanya's murder.

"As well as can be expected. I need to see Seth right away. We'll talk more when I get back, okay?"

"I'll hold you to that."

I nodded and left. I set out down Front Street toward Cold Feet Café. I'd scratched Big Finn from my list of those I could ask about the murder. He was likely consoling Meg. But there was always Zelda. Someone bumped into me. I uttered, "Excuse me."

"Oh, Daryl Anne, I'm so glad to run into you."

I glanced at the person attached to the voice and did an inward groan. Lila Spiboda, aka Spybody, the town gossip, er, I mean librarian.

"This murder has the town in an uproar," she said, then began clicking off questions with the speed of an auctioneer. "Did you see it happen? What was it like seeing a dead body? How did the guests react? How is Meg doing? Who do you think did it? I heard your mother got into a row with Tanya at The Last Fling tavern the night before. Is Susan a suspect?"

"No. What an awful thing to say." The bottom dropped out of my stomach. Oh, God. That was the last thing I wanted to hear. "And don't spread rumors like that."

I crossed the street and began to run, away from the wedding shoppers and curiosity-seekers, away from Spybody. Thankfully this street was devoid of other curious Weddingville citizenry.

Seth's studio was a block off the waterfront, in what had once been the porch and living room of his parents' Craftsman-style house. The senior Quinlans were retired, traveling with a group of friends in their RVs, seeing America. Seth's brothers worked in the area, but neither had had the eye for photography that

Seth inherited from his father, and for now, at least, he lived in the house alone.

At least, he'd been alone last time I was in town. Loud barking told me that was no longer the case. From the noise, I expected a puppy to fly at me when Seth answered my rings, but instead a fully grown golden Lab greeted me. Seth held him by the collar. "Sit, Sonny."

The dog complied, tail wagging, eagerness in his dark eyes. I held my hand out for him to sniff, then stroked the top of his head. "A new friend?"

"Yep. A rescue buddy."

Our gazes met, his warm and full of light. I asked, "He need rescuing or you?"

Seth grinned, and my knees turned to mush. "A little of both, I think. This big, old place was feeling empty."

Empty = lonely. I knew that feeling.

"Come on in. The coffee's fresh, and the inhabitants are fresher."

Was he flirting with me? Or just teasing me as usual? I could tease too. "A long as fresh doesn't mean ripe…"

He laughed as I stepped across the threshold. I followed him through the darkened studio and into a wide-open family room and kitchen full of natural light and breathtaking water views. "Wow. You remodeled."

Had I been out of town that long? Yes, I suppose I had.

"Yeah, took down a couple of walls and opened it up." He asked, "Do you approve?"

"Very much." The once-galley kitchen was gone. The new kitchen was sleek and modern with white cabinets, a large island, stainless appliances, and hardwood floors throughout. A round table that could accommodate twelve filled a bay window with views to the water. The main seating area was burgundy leather, consisting of two massive chairs and a sofa centered around a brick fireplace with a big-screen TV atop a huge driftwood mantel.

"I was just looking over some of the shots I took at the wedding."

Good timing, Blessing. I'd been wondering how to breach the "cause of death/time of death" subjects, but he'd given me the perfect opening. And yet, I was biting my lower lip, Meg's trait, not mine. When had I started doing that?

"I take it you saw the special edition of the paper?" The smile fell from his rugged face, his expression growing as somber as the topic.

I nodded. "Yeah, I did."

"I only know what's in the *Weekly*."

"If you came here looking for more information, then you're about to be disappointed. I'm not allowed to divulge anything I know or suspect."

My hopes dropped. "Not even how Tanya was murdered?"

"Not even. Not until the autopsy results are in and made public."

"Even if I swear not to tell another living soul?"

Seth poured me coffee and handed me a mug that bore his logo. He ignored my wheedling. "Although I did get an update on Reverend Bell."

Oh, God. I grimaced, contrition burning my cheeks. I'd been so upset about the murder that I'd totally forgotten about the minister. "Is he okay?"

"He will be."

"Was it a heart attack or stroke, then?"

"Neither. He was drugged."

"Drugged? Self-inflicted?"

"I doubt it. Sleeping pills in his herbal tea. Not enough to kill him, just enough to knock him out. By the time the ceremony started, the effects were taking place. It's why he was slurring his words and swaying."

I hadn't noticed the swaying. "I thought maybe he'd been drinking or was doing recreational drugs, and when he collapsed, well…I assumed the cause was one of those."

"Giving the minister an overdose of sleeping pills is as effective a way as any to stop a wedding," he said pointedly.

If you don't stop this wedding, I will. My chest seemed to fill with ice. "Was Tanya's body coming ashore also part of the plan to stop the wedding?"

"I don't believe the two are related," he said, the answer coming so quick that I knew he'd been mulling this over. "Seriously. There weren't any boats in that stretch of water all morning. So what are the odds that a body dumped farther up shore would end up where and when it did?"

I couldn't do the math required to answer that. I shrugged, in case he could.

"Besides," he started, but broke off just as abruptly, a crooked smile parting his sexy lips. "Whoa. Damn, Blessing, you're good. Getting me to let down my guard and spill my guts. I'm going to have to watch myself around you, aren't I?"

Definitely flirting. Why did I have to like that so much? Why did I wish he'd do more than flirt? Why did my insides suddenly feel like melted gold, liquid and hot? I strove for an innocent expression. "What do you mean?"

"I told you that I can't discuss this with you."

I hated roadblocks. I sighed and tried another tact. There had to be a loophole or two in whatever agreement he had with the

Weddingville Police Department. "Is there some rule that says we can't speculate on what happened?"

He sipped coffee, chocolate eyes locked with mine, but I could tell he was rolling around my suggestion. "I guess not."

"Well, then...?"

His grin broadened, and he stared at my mouth as if he wanted to kiss me. The wayward thought made my mouth water. He said, "You have to swear on Billie's life that you won't tell anyone this, not even Meg."

"Cross my heart. Pinkie swear."

He ignored my little finger, studying me a long moment, as if trying to decide whether or not to trust me. I almost laughed. He had to know with my giveaway face that he'd be able to tell immediately if I were being insincere. Obviously I'm not a good liar. But perhaps he didn't know that a pinkie swear was as good as an unbreakable pre-nup.

He made up his mind and invited me to sit at the table. His laptop was there, tempting me to spin it my way so that I could check out the photos he'd taken. Wait. Did I really want to view a murdered body up close? No. I breathed easier when he shut the laptop. We sat next to each other, Sonny nosing in between, placing his muzzle on Seth's thigh.

"This has nothing to do with cause of death." Seth stroked the dog's head. "It's only speculation on my part. As I said, I've been viewing the photos this morning. I noticed something...odd. I thought a strip of seaweed had gotten wrapped around Tanya's waist, but the more I looked at it today, the less certain I was. So I blew up the frame. Turns out, it was some sort of cloth or ribbon."

Like a certain missing cloth belt? My deepest fear reared its ugly head. I glared at Seth's laptop. My alter ego, Ms. Denial, came to my rescue. "Anything could have snagged on the body while it was in the water, right?"

He frowned, as if debating the wisdom of telling me what he was thinking. For two seconds, I fought the urge to run, but his words riveted me to the chair. "More like the killer used it to attach a weight of some kind so that the body would sink."

I felt the blood drain from my face and congeal in my tummy. "Of course. That makes more sense." Had someone used my mother's belt to insure Tanya's body would stay underwater forever? If so, why? The obvious reason sickened me. To incriminate her, of course. Oh God, was that what had happened? *No. Calm down, Daryl Anne.* "But wouldn't it make more sense to use a rope or heavy-duty twine to keep the body from ever surfacing?"

"It would have. But this smacks of using what was at hand."

The air seemed to vanish from the room, and a lump the size of Sonny's toy ball clogged my throat.

"Are you okay? You look kind of ill."

Like the time you spun Meg and me in the teacup ride at the carnival when we were kids, and I literally turned green just before tossing my cookies? That was exactly how I felt now. Any lie about "feeling okay" wasn't going to fly. "This…this should have been such a joyful homecoming…"

He sighed, the sound as heavy as my thoughts. "Definitely not the usual Weddingville wedding."

He reached over, his big hand covering mine. The touch was reassuring and intimate, robbing some of the sense that I was alone in a scary new world. Reminding me the new world held other things, like feelings for a man I didn't dare encourage, yet couldn't stop craving. I let the warmth filter through my being.

But my mind—perhaps still seeking any explanation that didn't involve my mother tossing Tanya's body into the water—refused to wander from the subject at hand. "Any substantial weight attached to a dead body would take someone super strong, or even two people, to toss it into the water. Right?"

He rubbed his chin, taking a second to consider that. "Depends on where the murder occurred. There are some pretty high cliffs around here, where the water remains deep despite the flux of the tide. One person could roll a body off such an edge without lifting it."

Which meant even a woman could have dumped Tanya into the sound. A black cloud appeared on the horizon of my hopes. I prayed for a strong gust of clarity to blow it away. I needed to disconnect my emotions and look at what I knew, and not keep working up scenarios of unacceptable possibilities. More facts would help. "It's just so odd that the body ended up on the beach by the gazebo of all places."

Seth frowned. "It is odd, but I assume the sheriff will check with the local NOAA about tide flow and currents."

"NOAA?"

"National Oceanic and Atmospheric Administration."

I drained my mug. I thought I'd feel better after talking to Seth. Instead, I was quaking in my boots. I shouldn't have put off talking to Mom. "I wish you'd tell me how she died."

He sipped his coffee, studying me and my readable face. "What's going on Blessing? What has you nibbling that gorgeous lower lip?"

"Nothing," I lied. Had he called my lower lip gorgeous? He had. My pulse picked up. I wanted to crawl into his lap and let him hold me, kiss away my concerns, make love to me until the sheer pleasure of it erased everything dark from my mind. *Oh,*

God. Don't let that be written on my face. I bit my lip harder. "Nothing."

"I see." He pitchforked his fingers through his thick, tawny hair. "You want me to share what I know or suspect, but you aren't willing to offer me the same in return."

Guilty as charged. If this kept up, I'd wear a hole in my lower lip. "Who do you think vandalized the wedding tent and sent that note?"

My sudden switch of topics wasn't lost on Seth. He recognized the diversion tactic for what it was and rolled his eyes. "And drugged Reverend Bell?"

"Yeah. Did Troy mention any leads on that?"

"If he did, I wouldn't tell you."

I nodded, not feeling less guilty about holding out on him. He was working with the police. Best not to share my worries about Mom and the soiled dress. The missing belt. Not now. I wanted the facts first. And when I had them, I might never tell Seth. It depended on what I learned.

This time Seth changed the subject. "Have you spoken to Meg?"

I rolled my neck, the tightness there starting to give me a headache. "Not yet. Either she's misplaced her phone again, or she has it turned off. I'm not sure where she is. I figured I'd swing by the café after I leave here. See if Big Finn knows where I can find her."

"Sounds like a plan. I'd like to go with you, if you'll wait for me to e-mail the file photo to Gooden. Sonny hasn't had his morning walk yet."

"I'd like the company." Anything to ease the nagging worry about that missing dress and my mom's avoidance of me. This was the first time I could recall that she hadn't texted or called me at least twice a day. Even when I was in town. Yes, the bridal season was on, and the shop teemed with alterations and appointments and walk-ins, but that had never mattered. She always wanted to touch base with me. I felt as if I'd been cut adrift, my lifeline severed. Knowing my mother, she'd done this for my sake, thinking she was doing what was best for me. I'd never suspected she was a person to run from the truth. Or to hide from it. But what else could I think now?

The thought stopped me cold. I had been doing a lot of that lately, myself. *Run, Daryl Anne, run. Hide. Deny. Apparently, I'd inherited the distasteful trait.*

* * *

As we approached Cold Feet Café, I recalled Tanya telling me about the diner's first days. No customers. Food wasted. The sinking feeling that they would lose everything they owned. Apparently nothing was as good for business as the murder of one of the former co-owners. There wasn't a seat in the house. Folks were wedged tighter than sardines in a can. "I'm pretty sure they've exceeded their occupancy limit."

"No kidding." Seth held tight to Sonny's leash, the dog lured by the delicious aromas wafting out to us through the rooftop vents. "I don't think I've ever seen more people in the café than on the street."

"There aren't more people than on the street," I said, glancing at the myriad shoppers milling along the sidewalks.

"I dunno…it's a zoo in there."

"It's a zoo out here," I said. I focused on the café, my confidence slipping away. "I doubt I'll find Meg here." *Or Big Finn.* Through the café window, I saw a gossipy friend of Billie's spot me. An uneasy sensation raised the hair on my nape as she tapped her companions on the shoulder, and one by one they turned in my direction. "I need to get to the shop. Thanks for… everything."

I started to move even as he stared at my lips, seeming reluctant to part with my company. But the old ladies were getting to their feet, tossing money at the counter, starting for the door. Panic swept me.

"Okay. See you later?"

"Sure. Call."

As Seth and Sonny headed down to the beach trails, I spun to hurry off, but wedding shoppers crowded the sidewalk, impeding a speedy escape. I'd only made it as far as *The Flower Girl* florist shop when Billie's friends caught up with me. Velda Weeks, the most aggressive of the trio, snagged hold of my arm. Around five-four and shrinking, she was panting, her age-spotted hand on her hip. Her boobs drooped southward toward her belt, a fact made more evident by her lack of a bra. She claimed that particular undergarment caused her untold shoulder pain and did nothing to improve the status of her *girls*.

"Daryl Anne," she huffed. "We are so glad to run into you."

Run after me, you mean. I refrained from saying it.

Jeanette Corn, lean as a dock post, nodded. She'd wound her long, gray braid around the top of her head like a garland, a hairdo she'd worn since the seventies. *Long live Woodstock.* "I told Velda, if anyone would be able to give us the real scoop, it would be you."

"What scoop?" I asked, feigning complete ignorance. They wanted the same thing I'd gone to Seth to get. Facts.

"Don't go all zippy-mouthed on us, Daryl Anne Blessing," Wanda Perroni warned, shaking a finger at me as if it we were standing in the kitchen of her Italian bakery and that finger were a wooden spoon. "We used to change your diapers, you know."

Was that supposed to be a bargaining chip? I bit down a smile and started walking. "I'm needed at the shop."

Velda still had a grip on my forearm and was forced to move with me. "We won't keep you but a minute."

"Then get to it, Velda," Wanda said. "The girl hasn't got all day, now does she?"

"Right as usual, Wanda." Velda yanked on my arm, and like a dog on a leash, I was forced to stop or end up tripping her. She leaned in, giving me a whiff of the cabbage she'd cooked that morning. "Since you were there and all, we figured you'd have the scoop."

Again with the scoop.

"Did Meg's mother die at the ceremony?" Jeanette blurted.

The question filled my head with sickening images, and my stomach pinched. Oh, brother. I could lie—oh, how I wanted to lie—but my telltale face would give me away. That didn't mean I couldn't hedge a little. "Not exactly."

"Not exactly?" Wanda frowned. She knew a runaround when she heard it. "Is the woman dead or not?"

"She is." I bit my lower lip. "But she didn't exactly die *at* the ceremony."

"*The Weekly* claims she did." Velda huffed.

Jeanette's hands went to her hips. "The paper says she was murdered right there."

"I read the account today, too, and it does not say that."

"Then where was she murdered?" Wanda demanded.

I gaped at her, frowning so hard that pain etched through my skull as shoppers bumped against our little group. "How should I know?"

"Well, you were at the wedding," Velda said, as if that meant I could answer all the who, why, where, what, and how questions that only the murderer knew.

"Look, ladies, the police are still looking into it, and they aren't giving out details."

"Yes, but you were there," Wanda reiterated.

I sighed. I wasn't getting free until I gave them something. I decided to keep it to a verifiable fact. "I don't have any juicy insider details. All I know is that her body washed ashore."

"I was right," Wanda said, wearing an I-told-you-so smirk.

Jeanette crossed herself.

But Velda looked as if she'd been sucking on sour grapes. "Well I, well I—I just never. Was she shot or strangled or drowned or poisoned?"

"Don't know."

Wanda shook her head. "My bet's on strangled. Seems like lots of folks wanted to do that to her."

Jeanette and Velda nodded in agreement. Jeanette said, "Not that the vile creature, God rest her soul, didn't court such a fate. But the least she could've done was think about her daughter."

In other words, how rude of Tanya for being killed and not considering first that she might wash ashore during Peter and Meg's wedding? "Um, I don't think she had any say in where her body was dumped."

"All the same. It was in very poor taste." Velda sniffed, disapprovingly, and finally released her hold on me. "Give Billie and Susan our best, dear."

The trio shuffled off toward the café, heads together, undoubtedly deciding which salacious bits to mete out to the other gossipers awaiting their update.

There was no relief at the bridal shop. It, too, was packed with curious Weddingville residents, none of whom were shopping for wedding attire, but who were asking after me. I had to get out of there. Now. But that proved easier said than done. A swirl of bodies impeded my progress to the main door, bumping and spinning me this way and that. As I neared my objective, I caught my mother's reflection in a mirror. It was an unguarded moment. There was a strange desperation in her eyes and an angry scratch on her cheek.

Chapter 13

I exited the bridal shop, emerging into the warm day, feeling chilled and lost, much like the day my dad died. I started walking, heading to my quiet place without even thinking about it. A lone figure sat at the end of the dock. I recognized that fiery red hair that now seemed like flames against the murky water in front of her. Meg.

Meg wore faded jeans and a plaid shirt that I knew belonged to her father. A scrunchie that she must've had since junior high was as ineffective now as it had been then in taming those wild tresses. I started toward her. Seagulls cried overhead like a chorus of mourners, covering my best friend's grieving sobs and the sound of my steps. But Meg felt the footfalls tremor through the dock planking as I approached. She lifted her head, on alert, ready to ward off anyone with nerve enough to invade her private retreat. Until she saw it was only me. Without a word, she scooted over, and I sank down beside her. I waited. Nothing I could say would ease this heartache. I knew. I'd lived it.

It had been enough that Meg sat with me when I was at my lowest point. She'd offered me chocolates and condolences. I had no candy, but prayed my being here would offer her at the least a modicum of that same comfort. As her sobs began to subside, I found the small packet of tissues in my pocket and offered one, then another. She blew her nose, wiped her damp cheeks, sniffled, and took my hand. I squeezed.

She held on tight and said, "This was definitely not the wedding I dreamed it would be."

The pronouncement came with a wobbly smile that stabbed my heart. "I'm sorry."

"The last thing I said to her was so... mean."

I squeezed her hand again, wishing I was brilliant and had a magic wand to vanquish the guilt edging that confession. "I'm sure she knew you didn't mean it."

"But I did." Contrition filled Meg's watery gaze. "That's the awful thing. I did mean it. She didn't love me. She only came here to horn in on my future life with Peter."

Sometimes I hated being right.

Meg grimaced. "So why am I so sad?"

A weight settled on my chest. "Because you're a good person, and you wouldn't have wished what happened to her."

"No. I wouldn't." We fell silent for a long stretch. Meg pulled out the scrunchie and rewrapped it around a handful of hair, the result a crooked ponytail. "I can't figure out who in this town hated her so much they would've killed her."

Whereas I could think of several folks with motive. Including me. "I have it on good authority that she was kicking up her heels at The Last Fling after the rehearsal dinner broke up."

"Must have been after I told her to get lost."

Licking her wounds? Drowning her sorrows?

"Who was this good authority?" Meg asked.

"Who else?" I grimaced at the memory. "Spybody."

"It must be true then." Meg's frown was indicative of someone weighed down with a boatload of unanswered questions.

Maybe I watched too many mysteries on TV or maybe it was working in Hollywood, but my mind veered into detective-think. "It's not impossible that she could have hooked up with some lowlife at the bar. Are the police only looking for suspects among those who knew her? Are they even considering that it might have been a random crime?"

"The sheriff didn't mention anything about The Last Fling..." Meg said, perking up at the suggestion. A look I recognized brightened her eyes.

"Are you thinking what I'm thinking?"

She began to nod, reading my mind as only a best gal-pal can. "I've developed a powerful thirst sitting here in the sun. I could really use something to wet my whistle."

* * *

The Last Fling sat several blocks out of town in a nonresidential area. It was, I realized, very near the cliffs that Seth had suggested might've been where the body was dumped into the bay. I shivered, even as an odd sense of excitement skittered through me. Coming here felt right. Yet a little dangerous. We might be onto something.

The parking lot was compacted dirt that turned into a muddy bog whenever it rained and a dust bowl during long, dry patches of good weather. We parked amid a slew of other cars and a couple of motorcycles and let the dust billows settle as we eyed the bar from the safety of the windshield. Once a lumberman's lodge, the log building backed against a stand of Douglas fir, new growth that had replaced the original trees used as material to build this place. Everything about it screamed lumberjack and biker gang hangout, except the frilly painted sign.

But the name change wasn't the only concession the bar owner had made to the city council's mandate for wedding-themed uniformity. The ceiling had once displayed dozens of hats, mostly baseball caps, but those had been replaced by garters. Blues garters, pink and white garters, red garters, and even one black garter. I glanced toward the stage, saw the featured band was Bridey and the Grooms. Playing nightly.

As music and chatter swirled around us, I took in the customers with one sweep. If this were an episode of our sitcom, I would've chosen biker-bar-chic or cowboy work clothes for cast members. These patrons, however, wore a variety of jeans or Bermudas, tank tops or polo shirts, and boaters or flip-flops. A trendy couple near the door dined on shrimp cocktails floating in a watery red sauce.

The music started up again, then stopped. I glanced toward the stage at the band and did a double take, realizing that I knew the blue-haired singer. Jade Warren, bridesmaid number two. I nudged Meg in the ribs and whispered, "I thought Jade said her band was called The Jaded Edge."

"It is." Meg nodded. "They have upcoming gigs booked in Las Vegas."

"Really? Then what are they doing here calling themselves Bridey and the Grooms?"

Meg's gaze followed mine to the dance floor, and her head snapped back fast enough to induce whiplash. "What the heck…"

"She lied to us," I said.

"No. Maybe they're just using this place to rehearse the material for their Vegas shows." Meg frowned, obviously wanting to deny what was right in front of her. She trusted people too easily. But faced with the proof, she abandoned the denial as fast as makeup that had reached its expiration date. Meg said, "Yeah, she lied to us."

I sighed. We both knew why Jade had lied. Back in our high school days, the three of us shared our ambitions of showbiz careers. Now Meg and I were living in L.A., working at a Hollywood studio on a popular TV sitcom. Meg was about to marry a movie star. Luck had been less kind to Jade.

Luck needed a swift kick.

My neck itched, that creepy crawling sensation of being stared at. But glancing surreptitiously around, I realized it wasn't just one person boring a hole in my back. It was pretty much everyone. The guys playing pool, the guys playing darts, the guys guzzling beer at a nearby table, the bartender, the waitress. Everyone except the bald, head-down drunk at the end of the bar. I cringed.

Usually when we drew male interest, drinks would arrive at our table, followed shortly by sex-minded dudes offering cornball pickup lines. Compared to this, that was a cakewalk. These stares hurt my heart. They were for the bride whose wedding ceremony ended with her mother's corpse washing ashore. No one approached us. But I could tell they wanted to. The air actually vibrated with collective curiosity and with the restraint the curious showed in leaving us alone. Bravo for good manners. And the difficulty of knowing what to say to Meg in this situation.

"The last thing I want to do is embarrass Jade," Meg said, backing toward the exit. I wasn't entirely sure it was only Jade that worried her. "We should leave."

"No." I knew I was being cruel asking Meg to stay and risk ending up the target of thoughtless remarks or questions, but she wanted answers as much as I did. "If Jade was playing here that night, we need to find out whatever she can tell us."

Meg messed with her scrunchie again, as though tightening it somehow tightened her resolve. "You're right."

I didn't have a scrunchie to tweak my courage. I'd have to get my bravado the tried and true way, from a bottle. *Sometimes only old school works.* "Let's get a drink."

We bellied up to the bar. I wanted a straight shot that would sear through my middle and burn up the ball of anxiety singeing my solar plexus. But I wasn't an it's-noon-somewhere drinker. We each ordered a Honeymoon Sweet, Irish coffees, light on the Irish, heavy on the whipped cream. Pool balls clinked amid occasional laughter. The band continued tuning, doing rifts, and stopping a song in the middle a couple of times. Jade's voice had matured, acquired a lilting vibration over the years that felt like honey in my ears. Rich. Smooth. Addictive. I'd buy her CD in a heartbeat. But the song was unfamiliar, something about broken dreams and empty roads ahead. Had she written it herself?

"Wow, she still has that amazing voice, only somehow it's even better," Meg said. "She's wasted doing gigs in dives like this."

"We both know how difficult it is to break into the music business," I said, reminding her of other friends we shared who couldn't get seen or heard by any recording honcho. "The streets of Hollywood are paved with brokenhearted, mega-talented artists."

"She ought to try out for one of those shows like *The Voice*." Meg licked whipped cream from her upper lip. "She's good enough to win or at least gain recognition, which could lead to a break."

I had a thought. "Maybe you could take a demo tape to Peter's agent?"

Meg lifted her head, smiling. "I could do that. Let's go tell her."

"Not now. We don't want to interrupt—" As I said that, the music stopped. Voices filled the gap. No one applauded. And the sadness I'd set aside momentarily seemed to increase. Meg had lost her mother. Jade's incredible talent was going unappreciated. Both sorrows weighed heavy on my heart. We couldn't save Meg's mom, but maybe we could do something to help Jade.

I finished my coffee, and as I lowered the mug, my gaze met Jade's in the mirror. "What are you two doing here?"

Meg and I spun on the stools at the same time. Jade's shoulders were as squared as a defensive end from my favorite football team, the Seattle Seahawks. I said, "Meg had to get out of the house."

My best friend nodded. "Walls closing in."

The tightness around Jade's mouth softened. She gave her long hair a toss, causing the blue streak to bounce like a loose ribbon. "I'm sorry, Meg. I liked your mom, you know."

"Thanks."

"Do the police have any idea yet what happened?" Jade asked, the question everyone in the room wanted to ask.

Before Meg could respond, I said, "We heard Tanya was here after the rehearsal dinner broke up."

"So?" Jade's animosity showed as her gaze shifted in my direction. Like adopted cats who share the same space, we tolerated each other out of our mutual respect and affection for Meg.

"Were you here too?"

Her chin came up. "What if I was?"

Meg—probably sensing an impending dustup—jumped in. "Jade, you have a truly awesome voice. Do you really have gigs booked in Vegas?"

Jade reined in whatever storm she'd been about to unleash on me, but her nostrils still flared. She gave Meg her full attention and a non-answer. "Why?"

"It's not a trick question," I said. "Are you or aren't you booked in Vegas?"

She cut me a glare. "My agent is working on it."

"Oh, darn," Meg said. "Then you have an agent already."

Jade blinked. "Already?"

"Well, I thought, I mean, really it was Daryl Anne who thought, that if you didn't have an agent or other representation maybe I could get Peter's agent to listen to a demo CD. You know, to help you get in front of the right people."

Jade flipped her hair again. "This was Daryl Anne's idea?"

I hoped my giveaway expression said that I wasn't half the bitch she thought I was. Instead, I saw something flash through her gaze that shouldn't be there. Regret? Shame? Self-reproach? I couldn't be sure which, and I hadn't a clue why such a generous offer would cause her to feel any of those emotions.

"I do have a demo CD. In my bag, actually." She pointed to a table in the corner where a large hobo-style purse perched. She stepped up to the bar and ordered a beer. Once she'd secured it, she gestured for us to join her at her table. As we walked over, she said, "I really did think your mom was a kick, Meg, but honestly, from what I observed, I might've been in a minority."

"It's okay," Meg said, swallowing hard and twisting the scrunchie again.

I feared a meltdown in the making. If we were to get through without that, I had to take charge and stay on task. *Just the facts, ma'am. Yes, I learned my detecting skills from TV. Don't judge. It's the best I have.* I pinned Jade with a glance. "Did you notice if Tanya came in alone that night?"

She started to bristle, an automatic reflex, but caught herself. She downed a swig of beer. "She wasn't alone. And even if she had been, she wouldn't have been for long. She was a party-starter, you know? When she showed up, the joint got hopping."

No denying that. "Who did Tanya come in with?"

"That camera dude with the strange eyes."

My heart tripped and I blurted, "Seth?"

"No. The one she worked with."

"Kramer." If he had a first name, I'd never gotten it. I couldn't reconcile Tanya going out with her cameraman. He'd bolted from the rehearsal dinner shortly after his rant to me. Had he been the vandal who'd destroyed Meg's wedding? Nah. He'd more likely have found himself a hiding spot to secretly film the whole affair to sell to the tabloids. "How were they getting along?"

"They weren't. He didn't stay long. They seemed to have a spat of some kind. I was on stage. I could see them, but was too far away to hear the argument. But just before he left, he shouted, 'I'm leaving. See you in Tinsel Town, bitch.'"

"Then he left before the wedding?"

"I guess. I didn't see him at the ceremony," Jade said.

"Therefore not under the sheriff's orders to stay in town," I murmured, wondering if he'd somehow managed to skip out after the murder. Or if he'd actually stormed out of here, checked out of his motel, and hightailed it to the airport as he'd implied. Gone. Before Tanya was killed.

Jade dug a CD out of her hobo bag and gave it to Meg, thanking her for the opportunity, forgetting that I'd suggested it. She reassured Meg that she had no expectations, but appreciated the chance. I caught that strange look in Jade's eyes again. Definitely guilt. And regret. As if she were doing something, or had done something, that she was kicking herself for now.

Meg scooted her chair back. "I need to hit the ladies. I'll be right back."

I almost went with her, but Jade's hand landed on my arm. She mouthed, "Stay."

The moment we were alone, she said, "I didn't want to ask this in front of Meg, but is it possible that Peter knew her mother before coming to Weddingville?"

Worry about my mother's strange behavior since the night of the rehearsal dinner had temporarily purged the conversation I'd overheard. And Kramer's bombshell. But the memory sprang at me now like a rattler, with biting recall, bringing back all the intensity and venom of the moment. Peter warning someone, probably Tanya, *"If you say one word about that to Meg, I'll kill you."*

My mouth dried. "What makes you ask?"

She glanced toward the restrooms, watching out for Meg. "I stayed and had a drink after the last set that night. As I was leaving, I spied Tanya outside, talking to someone parked near the end of the building. Back by the woods. She was standing next to his car. He had the driver's door open, a leg hanging out. It was a man. I'm not sure that it was Peter, but it was definitely that fancy car of his."

The Honeymoon Sweet curdled in my stomach. What were the chances of two tan Jaguars bearing California license plates being in town that night? With someone at the wheel who knew Tanya? A gazillion to zero. This information could get my mother out of the frying pan, but it would put Meg's fiancé directly into the fire. I wasn't sure she could deal with another kick in the heart. "Did you tell this to the police?"

"Sheriff Gooden hasn't questioned me yet," Jade said, frowning.

And I was sure that Peter wasn't going to volunteer it.

"I'll have to tell the sheriff, won't I?" Jade looked horrified by the thought, as if she also realized what it would do to our mutual friend.

"Why don't you tell me instead," a male voice said from behind us. Jade and I jumped in our chairs like birds startled off a perch. Troy. As handsome in his uniform as Meg had claimed and even more formidable. His dark expression looked explosive, but he'd keyed into the roomful of onlookers and kept his voice to a low growl. "And then you can tell me what the hell you think you're doing interfering with a police investigation."

"It's not like I was hiding anything," Jade blurted, "I would have told you that I saw Peter talking to Tanya the night she was murdered as soon as the sheriff questioned me."

Too late I realized Meg was standing right behind Jade, her eyes as wide as portholes.

"Shit," Troy barked, spotting her, his scowl deepening. "You're in on this too?"

Chapter 14

Troy insisted Jade follow him to the station to take her statement.

Meg sat in the passenger seat of my mother's car looking confused and angry and scared as I drove us back into town. Despite my hope of sparing her more distress, she'd been handed a hard dose of it. I knew exactly what she was feeling. Peter was now a person of interest in the murder of her mother.

Meg yanked the scrunchie from her hair as if no amount of twisting or tightening could restore her peace of mind. "It couldn't have been Peter who Jade saw talking to my mother. It just couldn't. Why would he? What did they have to talk about?"

Was it time I 'fessed up about what Kramer had told me? About the conversation I'd overheard. About the threat? The thought of hurting her more stole my nerve. I should have mentioned it when Troy started questioning Jade, but I didn't want Meg to hear it that way. In front of others. The words froze on my tongue.

Meg shoved the scrunchie into her purse, absently opening a tiny container of balm and spreading in on her lips. "How would he even have known she was at The Last Fling? It's not like he'd give her his cell phone so that she could text him."

"Sweetie, as often as you misplace your phone, Peter's number might have gotten out to the whole town by now."

Even though I'd used my kindest voice, Meg blinked as if I'd slapped her. And I wanted to slap myself. I needed to tell her what I knew—which actually wasn't much if I broke it down. I couldn't prove Kramer's revelation was true. I didn't know if that was the secret Peter didn't want Meg to learn. Although I feared it might be.

I gathered every ounce of courage I could. "I haven't mentioned this to the police." Yet. "But earlier that night, at the rehearsal dinner, I overheard Peter threaten someone... probably, likely... your mother."

Her gaze stabbed me. "About what?"

"That's just it." I shrugged. "I don't know." I didn't. Not really.

"Maybe you misunderstood, then. Or maybe he was just teasing her."

Had she ever actually seen Peter tease anyone? Had Santa Claus grown wings and a tail? "He wasn't kidding."

She huffed. Meg didn't want to believe me, but it wasn't in her nature to leave it alone now that I'd presented it. "What exactly did he say?"

There was no way to soften the actual threat. No way to spare her whatever hurt it might cause to hear Peter's exact words. "Uh..."

"Tell me."

I did. And the color drained from her face. "What the hell is going on, Daryl Anne? I feel like I've stepped off the edge of the world. Like I'm floating in outer space with nothing to grab on to. No gravity in sight."

"I'm sorry." If Peter and Tanya had a past, he should tell her, not me.

She was silent all the way to her dad's house, then in a wobbly voice, she said, "Do you think Peter killed her?"

The fact that she'd allowed herself to even think that was hard enough to bear, but how much worse would it be if he'd had a fling with Tanya and he'd murdered her to keep it from coming out? But I couldn't say that to her. "I don't know."

"What could be so awful that he'd threaten to kill someone rather than tell me?"

"I don't know." I was starting to sound like a talking windup toy programmed to speak only one annoying phrase.

"I have to find out."

"I'm not sure you should ask your fiancé about this, Meg." *Until the police do.*

"Why not?"

Because if he knows that his secret is out, he'll just lie about what it is to cover his ass. "Because if he thought the secret was worth killing for once, he might—"

"Kill me?" Her voice came out a squeak. "Holy shit. You think he's guilty."

"I didn't say that..." But she was already hurrying up the walk toward her dad's house, moving as if she couldn't get away from me fast enough. I watched her go, kicking myself again for not handling that better. I didn't mean to offend her, just to caution her that Peter might be dangerous. He had a hair-trigger temper. I started to follow her, but thought better of it. Her state of mind wouldn't allow her to listen. I sat there, trying to figure out my next move. Should I call Troy? And say what? "I think Peter is a killer. Protect Meg." Troy would love any excuse to do just that. Still...

I reached for my cell, found the number, then hesitated. The main reason not to involve Meg's ex-boyfriend was that she'd be even more angry with me. Better to let her cool off. Think it through. Big Finn was home, greeting her in a bear hug, and pulling her inside. Comforted by the knowledge that he wouldn't let Peter do anything to harm Meg, I decided to go home and regroup.

I called Seth. He was as close as I wanted to get to the police at the moment. But he didn't answer. Frustrated, I disconnected and pulled away from the curb. I drove slowly up Front Street. Usually the sight of all the wedding-themed shops brought a lightness to my heart. It was like a mini-carnival with families and friends helping the bride plan the upcoming celebration.

But I realized as the car crawled along the street that something felt off-kilter. Less jovial. There were too many people milling about for a normal weekday. Parking spaces were nonexistent. Had these out-of-towners come for a purpose other than shopping for weddings? Had they come hoping to see where the murder of Peter Wolfe's future mother-in-law had taken place? Thrill-seekers. Vultures.

I wasn't getting sucked into this. I pulled into the reserved spot behind the bridal shop and started toward the back door. Darn. I'd taken Mom's spare key without noticing that it was the only key on the ring. The main salon was packed. I kept my head down and strode through the store and into the back room. Voices from within the sea of dresses slowed my steps. I crept toward the sound, caught by Billie's whispered words, "So you want to put this on hold for a few more months?"

"Do I have another choice?" *Zelda Love*. A loud sigh. "I begged him to tell Meg, but he said he didn't want to ruin her special day."

I halted. Confusion sifted through me. What secret did Zelda know that could've ruined Meg's special day? Had she also overheard Peter's threat at the rehearsal dinner? Or was this a different secret?

A rustle of fabric reached me, followed by the sound of a zipper.

"It's a shame." Zelda's voice broke.

"It is," Billie said. "This town could sure use some happy about now. Has the sheriff questioned you about Big Finn's whereabouts yet?"

"No. And I'm hoping he won't."

What did that mean? Did Zelda and Finn have something to hide from the sheriff? I stepped into view and spied Billie zipping up a dress bag that she'd placed on the hold rack. I asked, "Whatcha doing?"

Zelda and Billie jumped as only two caught in an act of secrecy could manage. Billie moved to block my view of the dress bag. "Nothing."

What was in the bag that she didn't want me to see?

"Hello, Daryl Anne." Zelda blushed, her hand fluttering to her neck. Except for the fluttery hand she looked so unlike herself I might not have recognized her if I hadn't heard her voice. Gone was the usual parrot-bright outfit I'd come to expect on her. Even her Crayola-yellow hair seemed zapped to a washed-out beige. Maybe it was the head-to-toe black she wore that gave her complexion that pasty hue. Or maybe it was Peter's secret. Or whatever she didn't want to tell the sheriff about Big Finn. Or about herself.

Anxiety gnawed my stomach. Too many people I cared about were going to be hurt if this murder wasn't solved quickly, and I didn't trust Sheriff Gooden to do the job.

The you-caught-us-doing something-look remained in Zelda's eyes, even as she said, "Your grandmother was just helping me rearrange some plans for my—one of my clients."

"That's right. Nothing you need to fuss about, Daryl Anne," Billie added, not meeting my gaze. Her tone was meant to squelch my curiosity. I was always amazed that she'd never quite glommed on to the fact that, invariably, this only made me more nosy. But not today. I had enough on my plate. I didn't care what they were up to. I was in mystery-solving mode.

"There you are," Seth said, walking into the storeroom. From the glint in his eyes, I was in trouble. He caught my elbow in a stage whisper and dragged me toward the doors that led into the office. "We need to talk."

Damn. Troy. He'd gotten to Seth before me. "I know Troy is pissed, but—"

"About what?" His brow arched. "I haven't spoken to Troy since I saw you last. Can we go somewhere alone?"

I didn't want to go anywhere, but upstairs to the Tylenol bottle. I felt tingling in my neck. I glanced behind us. Billie and Zelda, the two most ardent matchmakers in town, were following. Spying on us. I rolled my eyes. If I wasn't careful, they'd have us engaged and planning our wedding before the night was over. I cast an evil eye at Zelda's bulging notebook. She used one for each of her brides. The one she had with her today bulged a bit more than Meg's had. I shuddered at the possibility that my name—not some so-called customer's—was on that folder. Gooseflesh had me rubbing my arms. I wasn't staying in Weddingville. I wasn't marrying Seth. Although the thought sent an unbidden twinge of regret through my heart—which was strange considering we hadn't so much as kissed. "This way," I told him.

The elevator was compact, our bodies touching unavoidably, Seth's scent lacing every inhaled breath. And now I couldn't stop thinking about kissing him. Heat flushed through me. I tried looking everywhere, except those earnest eyes, that inviting mouth. It was useless. My gaze had a mind of its own.

"A penny for your thoughts," he said, his breath feathering my face.

He'd probably be shocked if I told him. Then again, why hadn't he ever tried to kiss me? I wanted him to kiss me. I wanted to kiss him. Without thinking about it, I did just that. It should have been the most awkward moment in my life. Instead, the quick touch of my mouth to his had the impact of an exploding dynamite cap. Electrodes shot through my bloodstream, setting nerves tingling in every inch of my anatomy.

He was startled when I pulled back as quickly as I'd attacked. "What did do that for?"

Pull back or kiss him? I decided he meant the kiss. No sense lying when he could read my face. "I've been wondering if I'd like it."

"And did you?"

His smirk set my heart thumping. But I made sure that wasn't written on my face. I shrugged. "Sure. What's not to like?"

"I liked it too, Blessing. But we can do better than that." He punched the stop button on the elevator, pulled me to him, and kissed me until my lips parted and his tongue invaded and sensations I'd never felt before swirled over me like delicious wisps of wind. My toes curled, my knees wobbled. It had been so long since I'd been with a man, I'd forgotten just how wonderful it could be.

My breath seized in my lungs. "Seth, I…"

He cut me off, his lips brushing mine again, and then touching his forehead to mine. "I've been wanting to do that since the other night."

I'd wanted to do that since junior high. Not that I could or would admit it. My pulse hummed with anticipation, even as I fielded regrets. I'd wondered what Seth would taste like for years, and now that I knew, I wished I could erase the knowledge and go back to ignorant bliss. I had no business encouraging anything further between us. I wasn't in love with Seth, just with the idea of him. He'd been a fantasy for too many years. Although I had to admit that the reality exceeded my imagination tenfold.

I dragged myself back to the moment. My head felt ready to crack open from too much tension. I preferred my drama on the small or big screen, not in real life, but it was the only way to change the mood. "Why did you need to talk to me?"

"I found out how Tanya died."

"You said you hadn't spoken to Troy."

"I didn't. I talked to the coroner. He wanted to see a couple of my photographs."

"How was she killed?"

"Strangled. Probably with that length of cloth around her waist."

The bottom dropped out of my stomach, and my heart crashed to my knees. I staggered, not from desire, but fear.

Seth caught me by the arm. "Are you okay? You look ill."

"Migraine." I grabbed the sides of my head. "Just need to lie down."

I started the elevator again, hit the down button. "I'll let you out the back door so you can avoid the worst of the crowds."

"I know. When did this peaceful little town become a circus parade?"

"Since a dead body washed ashore during a wedding. I can't wait to get back to L.A. and my normal life."

He looked crestfallen at the thought of me leaving. Or was I imagining it? He caught my head gently and kissed me tenderly. "See you later, Blessing."

I let him out. Then I stood there for a moment, waiting for the glow of my confused feelings about Seth to burn away the horror of my mother possibly being a murderer. Tanya had been strangled with the belt that belonged to the dress she'd thrown away. What other conclusion was there? Without realizing I'd been moving, I found myself in the storeroom, with rows upon rows of bagged wedding dresses. Maybe the dress wasn't thrown away, but rather hidden in plain sight. I pushed through the maze, the *swick* of plastic accompanying my hunt. Finally, I spied the hold rack.

My outstretched hand reached for the bag in question. Pain exploded in the back of my head. Stars danced before my eyes. My knees folded. I felt the floor looming toward me. Realized I was falling. As everything went black, I heard someone whisper, "Keep snooping and you'll be next."

Chapter 15

I'd pissed off a dangerous person. And I had no idea who. Fear took up residence in my heart. I jumped at every sound. Slept with the light on like after my dad died. Seth came by each night and double-checked every door and window in our building, making sure that locks were locked, giving me enough peace of mind that I could close my eyes without shaking.

Although the police were sympathetic, they had nothing to go on. Too many people had been in town that day and in the shop. Anyone could have crept into the storeroom and attacked me. But I knew it wasn't *anyone*. It was Tanya's killer. My only consolation was that the attack cleared away any doubt I harbored of my mother's possible involvement in Tanya's demise. Mom would never conk me on the head or threaten my life. She hadn't murdered Big Finn's ex-wife.

By day three of my recuperation, I was the pissed-off one. By playing the victim, hiding out in my room, and cowering at every creak this old building made, I'd given over my power to my attacker. I was taking it back. I dressed and made it as far as the sofa before the lingering effects of my concussion demanded I not take on too much the first day up.

Mom brought me a pillow and a fuzzy throw. "You rest awhile, sweetheart. I'll check on you around lunch time."

I snuggled into the cover, letting my mind drift. In my zeal to find evidence exonerating my mother, I'd stepped on the wrong toes. But whose toes? I mentally retraced where I'd been the days before the attack. Who had I spoken to? Who had I seen? Someone on the street? Someone at The Last Fling? I closed my eyes, picturing the bar's interior, scanning my memory to place the patrons. Nothing stood out.

I lifted my lids to find Meg kneeling by the coffee table. The air sizzled with an energy that seemed to emanate from her, as if she were plugged into an invisible socket.

"I've come to cheer you up," she declared, pointing to the compact makeup case on the tabletop. "You're entirely too pale. When I'm done working my sorcery, you'll dazzle."

"What if I don't want to dazzle?"

"Phooey. Who doesn't want to dazzle?" she asked with a lightness that I realized masked the turmoil she seemed to be feeling. This, I sensed, was more than mourning for a mother she'd never connected with and hadn't really known.

As she opened the case, I asked, "What's up, buttercup?"

"Nothing," she lied, gnawing her lower lip. She continued to stare at the products she'd brought as if weighing which of her magical beauty supplies to use first.

"Something," I corrected. "Out with it."

"Peter is pressuring me." She held an eyeliner brush like a wand. "His movie is starting. The police have given us permission to leave, and he wants us to fly to Las Vegas, get married, and go on to the set location in Dallas."

"Elope, huh?" Well, why not? The thought of another formal ceremony now stirred all sorts of disastrous memories for me, the drugged preacher, the murder. What must it do to her? Whereas Peter's suggestion accomplished the deed without a lot of trauma. Short, yet sweet. Then in a few months, the big, elaborate celebration party. So why wasn't Meg smiling or spilling over with excitement? "I take it you don't want to elope?"

She extracted a tub of lip gloss and one of her eye-shadow kits, finally meeting my gaze. "I promised myself I would not dump my problems on you."

Oh, brother. Only a doozy of a problem would move her to use that ploy. "What is it?"

She inhaled. "I finally told Peter."

I was used to her chaotic mind bouncing from one subject to another, and I could usually keep up without much trouble. But she'd lost me. "About...?"

"My feelings for Troy."

Whoa. That brought me upright. I shoved the throw aside, silently applauding her courage in facing her feelings. A marriage didn't stand a chance with lies and half-truths at the core. I was proud of her. "How exactly do you feel about Troy?"

She gave a toss of her head, the flame curls bouncing like indecision. "That's just it. I have serious, unresolved feelings for him. When I recall how it was between us, I still want to be with him. Forever. When I recall how he left, I don't want anything to do with him. Ever again."

"And you told Peter all of that?"

"Well, not exactly."

Good thing. "How did Peter take it?" Given his ego, not well would be my guess.

"Better than I thought he would. He said I needed time to regroup. That maybe I should stay with my dad while he went on to his movie set, and that I could join him there in a couple of weeks, and we could do the Vegas wedding then."

My mouth fell open. It's-all-about-me-Peter-Wolfe committing a truly selfless act filled me with disbelief. Had I misjudged him? Did he love Meg more than I gave him credit for? I couldn't equate this generous Peter with the threatening one. An ugly suspicion stirred. "Did he tell you what the secret was he didn't want your mother to tell you?"

She caught my chin to hold my head still while she began applying some cream or other to my eye area. "He said she was insisting he talk me into letting her walk me down the aisle along with Dad. You know, to give me away."

"If you say one word about that to Meg, I'll kill you." I recalled the anger in his voice and knew his explanation didn't ring true. It wasn't something over which someone would threaten murder. I closed my eyes as Meg applied liner to my upper and lower lids. Was I reading too much into what I'd overheard? Maybe. I might be taking threats a bit more seriously since being attacked. Right?

"Isn't Peter worried that you and Troy might…reconnect?"

Meg began using an eyeliner wand. I closed my eyes and listened to the dismay in her voice. "He said I just need to get Troy out of my system, and that he's sure when I spend some time around him again, I'll realize why we broke up. Something about leopards and spots."

Was Peter that trusting? Or was it that he believed that given a choice between himself and another man, a woman would always pick him? My vote? *Meet Hulk, the ego.*

"There," she said, handing me a mirror. "What do you think?"

I looked at my image, amazed that she'd managed to erase the signs of my restless nights and lack of sleep and restored me to my former self. "You're a wizard with makeup."

"I am," she said, turning introspective as she placed the brushes and tubes and pencils back into the case. "I don't want to give up my goal of one day owning my own salon."

"But as Peter's wife, you'll be able to afford a really incredible salon with a lot of employees and high-end clients."

"True, and I'm sure that's the only way Peter will really be onboard with my pursuing my dream. I've always wanted to own a high-end salon, but starting at the top seems wrong. I wanted to be hands-on with the customers, build the business slowly. Oh, I don't know. I just don't know."

"Then maybe staying here with your dad for a couple of weeks has more than one benefit. You'll be able to find your footing without all the distractions in L.A. or on a movie set, and then you'll be able to listen to your heart. That's how you'll figure out which direction is right for you."

She gave me a grateful smile and squeezed my hand. "Thank you."

"I'll bet your dad is glad you're staying on for a while. I imagine he's been pretty lonesome with you living in California."

Meg scrunched her face. "I think Dad might be hooking up with my wedding planner."

I stretched. "Um, Zelda told me they've been dating for about six months."

Her brows arched. "Well, that explains a lot. Why hasn't Dad told me?"

I shrugged. "Timing? Zelda said he didn't want to steal your thunder."

Meg smirked. "I think I almost caught her sneaking out of his bedroom this morning. She hurried outside to her car before we could speak. And when I asked Dad about it later, he…he blushed."

"What?" I'd seen Big Finn get red in the face for as many years as I could remember, but blush? Never. Could this be a serious romance? They were such opposites. She was as fluttery as a bird, and he was as down to earth as a tree. "She does seem to defuse his temper fairly easily. How would you feel about it, if you're right?"

Meg gave her long hair a flip. "I'd be glad for him. For both of them. He's been single for so many years. I was afraid he'd grow old and bitter and all alone. Especially when I marry Peter, since I'll be too busy to come home as often as I have been."

I let the idea of a Finn and Zelda romance filter through me and discovered the chill around my heart melting. A smile tugged. "I hope it's true."

"Me too."

"I hate to change the subject to a less palatable one, but have the police made any progress in Tanya's case?"

"I don't know." Meg put away the last of the makeup. "Troy won't discuss it."

Frustration bubbled to the surface and into my words. "There are a lot of people in this town with motivation, and unfortunately, they are all folks we care about. Your dad, my mom, Billie, even Troy." Maybe Peter. Even Zelda. "And if the murder is never solved, they will all live with the stigma of suspicion over their heads. Guilty by suspicion."

"Not to mention you always wondering if one of them brained you."

"The killer thinks I know something."

"Or that you're close to discovering something."

"If only."

"I think Jade is holding out on us," Meg said. "She looked guilty as hell when we questioned her at The Last Fling."

"I've been thinking the same thing."

"We should question her again."

But Jade wasn't at the bar when we arrived. She'd hooked up with Peter's agent and given her notice. I said, "That was quick."

"You heard Jade sing. Walter Fields is no fool. That was the act of an agent excited about a new, hot property."

"I wonder if she's left town yet?"

"I haven't heard."

We sat at the bar and ordered Honeymoon Sweets. I let the drink and the ambiance of the place invade my senses, hoping it would stir up a clear memory or two of who'd been here the day I was attacked. Nothing came. And yet, I had the niggling itch that I'd taken note of someone or something off-kilter that day. I just couldn't pull it to the surface.

"Fuck-a-duck, would you look at that!" the bartender roared, pulling me back to the moment. He was gaping at the TV behind us. He reached for the remote and cranked up the volume. "I'll be damned. Have you seen this?"

Meg and I spun around. My gaze flew to the wall-mounted wide-screen. A video was playing of our mothers in this bar, brawling like alley cats. Across the bottom, the ticker read: *Submitted by an observer who caught the whole thing on tape. A love triangle over twelve years old allegedly leads to murder.*

* * *

Meg dragged me out of The Last Fling, insisting she would drive. I didn't remember handing her my keys. I was shaking like a caught fish. "It's all over the news. And on the Internet thanks to that famous celebrity gossip site. Someone must have taped the fight with their cell phone or iPad."

"It looked more professional to me. No wobbly camera movements. Like the person doing the filming had experience filming such things. Like a professional or a paparazzo."

My brows lifted at the suggestion. "Like Kramer? Was he still in the bar when the fight occurred? According to Jade, he'd left before my mother arrived."

"Troy said he'd spoken to him in L.A. And Kramer sent the police proof that, when his flight was airborne, Tanya was still alive."

Disappointment flushed through me. "I guess I was really hoping he was the killer."

"That makes two of us. But don't let that video upset you. It might stir up suspicion, but given our moms didn't try to hide their animosity, I'd guess Susan is already on the list of possible suspects."

She hadn't meant to terrify me, but a raw, hot knot filled my stomach, making me feverish and chilled in equal turns. "What if the police see that video?"

"They probably already have."

She was right. I was burying my head in the sand. The need to find another, more solid suspect was the only excuse I had for immediately thinking of Peter. But God, how did I broach the subject when I didn't know the real secret Peter was keeping from Meg? Carefully. I realized there was another way to get what I was after. In a voice I reserved for kittens and babies, I asked, "Meg, what did you and your mother fight about?"

She frowned. "I told you. She wanted to horn in on my new life with Peter."

"No. What exactly did you say to each other?"

"Why?"

"Please, just indulge me."

Meg sighed. "I wanted to spare you."

"It's too late for that now."

"You're right. She tried to tell me that she didn't leave me of her own free will all those years ago. That she was run out of town by my dad and your mom and Billie."

The feverish sensation spiked higher. I feared my hair would spontaneously burst into flames. It was the same shit Tanya had accused my mother of. An accusation Mom hadn't denied.

Meg shook her head. "Don't worry. I didn't believe a word. She forgot that I was old enough to remember how she'd treated me."

I glanced at the houses as we passed, thinking what a serene little town this seemed, if one judged by its appearance and looked no further. So many secrets. So many lies. Half-truths. Meg had opened up to me. She deserved the same in return. I cleared my throat. "The night of the rehearsal dinner, my mom and Tanya had words. Tanya said some things about my dad. Hinted at an affair between them."

"Oh no. Did your mother punch her?"

"You saw the video."

As serious as this was, we nervous-laughed. Meg sobered first. "She denied it though, right?"

I shook my head.

"It can't be true," Meg said, climbing onto my denial bandwagon. I wanted to welcome her aboard, but I knew the horses pulling that particular cart were wearing out.

"I don't want to believe it either. But if there wasn't some grain of truth in it, why didn't she say so?" Why has she been avoiding me? Why did she hunt Tanya down at the bar and brawl with her? My mother wasn't a brawler. The video images flashed before my eyes, calling me a liar. At least I now knew how the dress got torn.

"I think it's time one of our parents told us the whole truth," Meg said, suddenly the logical, holding-it-together one. Me, falling apart like a seam with broken thread.

"There's something else I need to tell you first," I said. "I received a couple of threatening messages meant to stop your wedding." I told her the exact wording.

"Is that why the tent was shredded and splattered with blood?"

"Yes. And Seth told me that someone drugged Reverend Bell with sleeping pills so he'd fall asleep during the ceremony."

"Do you think the same person killed my mother?"

"No. Vandalism is one thing, threatening notes about stopping a wedding are mild compared to murder."

She considered a moment. "You think Troy did those things? He didn't want me to go through with marrying Peter. He wants us to give it another try."

I shook my head. "It's something he might've done before he joined the navy, but he's grown up. He's a police officer. He wouldn't risk his new career by breaking the law. And he wouldn't risk Reverend Bell's life."

"Then who would want to stop my wedding?"

I shrugged, "Your mother?"

"Why would she?"

The moment of truth. My mouth went dry. "She might've known Peter before coming to Weddingville. Or knew something he'd done that she didn't approve of and that she threatened to tell you about."

"You know what Peter said that was about."

"Meg, you don't threaten to kill someone just because they ask you to intercede on their behalf. Why wouldn't Peter just tell you that himself?"

She frowned as she pulled on to Front Street. "You're right. What is he hiding from me?"

We didn't have time to figure it out. Police cars were parked outside Blessing's Bridal. Meg parked. We ran to the front of the building to where a small crowd of onlookers had gathered. There were cameras flashing and people asking questions as Sheriff Gooden emerged with my mother in tow, her hands cuffed behind her. "Susan, did you kill Tanya Reilly Jones for stealing your husband?"

A buzzing sounded in my ears like a hundred bees. My head spun. I staggered. Strong arms caught me from behind, hauling me upright, holding on to me. I recognized Seth's cologne. For some reason that returned my strength. I shook free and tunneled through the crowd in time to see my mother's face peering out at me from the backseat of a squad car. She looked so helpless and afraid that I felt as if I'd been thrust into the role of parent. Reassuring words spilled out of me. "Don't worry. This is a mistake. I'll call a lawyer."

The police car pulled away from the curb. The press moved toward me like a swarm of vermin. Seth was there again, warding them off, protecting me. "No comment."

He hustled Meg and me into the bridal shop, then closed and locked the door.

We all startled at the gasp behind us. I pivoted and saw my grandmother standing there like a petrified tree. Her face was ashen, her lips blue, and she seemed to be sweating. "Billie are you—"

"I feel dizzy," she squeaked. Her eyes rolled back, and she went down, taking a mannequin with her.

Chapter 16

The bridal shop echoed with disturbing quietude, mannequins standing like forgotten soldiers on a frozen battlefield, silent witnesses as I placed the TEMPORARILY CLOSED sign in the storefront window. I had no choice. Mom in jail. Billie in the hospital. The media parked on our doorstep. What was I going to do?

Peter had offered to put up Mom's bail and hire her a top-notch criminal lawyer. Mom bolted at the idea of a stranger, even a rich one, bailing her out or hiring her a high-profile attorney. She insisted on court-appointed representation. No amount of arguing changed her mind. I couldn't make her understand how serious this was or how overwhelmed her wet-behind-the-ears public defender seemed.

Last night, I'd railed at Sheriff Gooden. "She didn't do this."

"The evidence says she did, Daryl Anne," was his only response.

Meg prevented me from doing something in the sheriff's office—to the sheriff—that I might later regret. I'd lost my normal calm, level-headed self, and Meg had found it. When had the world tipped on end?

Meg got me outside into the night, but I was still railing, "He's not going to keep looking into Tanya's death. He thinks he has the killer, but he's wrong." Cool, damp air caressed my face like a chilled cloth, lowering my internal temperature another few degrees. Any lower and I'd have hypothermia. "She didn't do this."

It was late afternoon the next day as I wandered aimlessly through the bridal shop's main salon, lost in dark thoughts. No solution in sight. I turned to find Meg there offering me a fresh cup of coffee. I thanked her, and the words slipped out, "Mom didn't kill Tanya."

"I believe you," Meg said, glancing sadly at the sign. She hooked her arm in mine, dragging me back through the silent shop to the elevator. "We need to find out who did before things go any farther."

Her dear face was so earnest that I thought my heart might explode with the blessing of her. How lucky was I to have a true friend? My sense of hopelessness lessened. "How are we going to do that?"

"Like I said before, it's time someone told us the truth about why my mother left town. And how your dad's death is connected to that." The second we reached the upstairs living quarters, she dug in her handbag, then patted herself down, finally rolling her eyes in exasperation. "Do you have your cell? I seem to have mislaid mine."

Surprise. Not. I handed over my phone. "Who are you calling?"

"Dad. Might as well get it from the horse's mouth." She pressed numbers. Listened. Disconnected. Repeated. "Darn. He's not at the diner or at home."

Disappointment made me frown. "And he doesn't own a cell phone."

She bit her lower lip. "Should I try Zelda's?"

Before I could answer, my phone rang. She handed it over. I read the screen, and my pulse kicked into high gear. "Gram? Are you okay?"

Billie's collapse had been a mild heart attack, brought on by a narrowed artery. A stent fixed the issue, but she'd also reinjured her wrist when she fell. The doctor insisted she remain in the hospital for a couple of days. To be safe. I suspected that he also didn't want her getting swept up in the craziness of what was going on with Mom. As if that could be avoided.

But it wasn't Billie on the phone.

"Ms. Blessing, this is your grandmother's doctor." He gave his name, but fear buzzed in my ears, and I didn't hear it.

"Is Gram—" The word stuck in my dry throat as my insides turned to liquid. "Okay?"

"Not really. I've instructed her that her recovery is reliant on the avoidance of stress, but she's very agitated. She insists there is something she must speak with you about in case she doesn't make it through the night. I've assured her that she is not dying and suggested putting off the visit for another day. However, she keeps pressing the matter."

That explained my stubborn streak.

"So I've reconsidered and think it might be best if—"

I interrupted. "Are you saying I should come to the hospital now?"

"Please." A relieved sigh filled my ear.

"On my way."

I explained to Meg what was going on, and she insisted on driving. She'd likely seen the tremble in my hand that I couldn't quite control and decided to remove the threat I would be to other drivers.

"Billie might know the answers to our questions," Meg suggested as we approached St. Joseph's Medical Center in Tacoma.

I tensed. Gram's ashen face flashed into my mind. I saw her collapsing again, and shivers raced through me. The idea of upsetting her sent a team of hungry rodents into my stomach. Could she fill in the blanks for us? Maybe. But… "We can't ask her. The doctor gave strict instructions that she can't be stressed, and the subject of Tanya always stresses her." More so now that Mom was behind bars.

"You're right. We won't bring it up. In fact, I'll just say 'hi' to her, and then go to the waiting area and keep trying to reach Dad."

She'd found her phone. That didn't mean it would still be on her when it was time to leave the hospital. "That sounds good."

But Gram wasn't having any part of Meg going to the waiting room. She took one look at us and began nodding. "Good. I'm glad you're both here."

She gestured us into the room. Her long black hair flowed loose around her shoulders, its unkempt state a sign that she wasn't one hundred percent herself. As if the cast on her wrist wasn't evidence enough. She'd raised the bed and was sitting up in anticipation of my arrival. "Pull up chairs and sit. I don't need fussed over."

It wasn't being fussed over that she disliked; it was having any medical issue that slowed her down or pinned her to a bed. If she were feeling slightly better, she'd commandeer us to abet her escape. But first we'd need to detach the beeping monitor and IV drip. On second thought, no thanks.

I went to the bed, kissed her cheek—which I was relieved to see had regained a normal pink hue. I squeezed her uninjured hand. "What is this I hear about you disobeying the doctor's orders?"

She ignored my tender reprimand. "Daryl Anne, I don't have much time. I suspect the doctor had the nurse put something to make me sleep in my IV drip. I could nod off at any moment. So let me do the talking."

I hid a smile behind my hand. "Okay."

"I assume you're extending your stay in Weddingville since Susan's gone and got herself in a pickle?"

"Of course." Much as I'd wanted to run back to L.A. that was out of the question now.

My answer smoothed the frown lines from between her eyes. "Good. There are three brides whose gowns and veils must go out this week. Check the calendar on my office desk for the names and phone numbers and reassure the brides that their dresses are ready for pick up. Two of the gowns are ready. The third, the one for the Millheimer wedding, needs to have the hem finished. I was working on it when the police came to arrest Susan. And," she waved the cast in the air, "I can't finish it. It's on my lounge chair in alterations."

"Okay, don't worry about it any longer. I'll handle it." Actually, I'd be glad for the mental diversion.

"Now, how's your mother doing?" Billie looked from me to Meg.

I hesitated, fearing I'd blurt out the dire situation in vivid detail. "She's not talking."

Gram shook her head and rolled her eyes. "I tried to get Susan to speak to you. Talked 'til I was blue in the face, but couldn't change her mind. She thinks her silence is protecting you."

The monitor beeped faster as her voice echoed my frustration. I wanted to ask, "Protecting me from what?" But knew not to agitate her further. "Gram, we can discuss this once you're home and recovered a bit more."

She shook her head again, muttering, "If Susan would've told you, told that fool sheriff, then I wouldn't be in this hospital bed."

You had a clogged artery. You would have had the attack sooner or later, I said inside my head. I didn't say it out loud. I'd been warned that she was doing the talking.

"I know Susan is still being tight-lipped. Otherwise she'd be here fussing over me." She tsked. "Sheriff Gooden's okay for keeping the peace, handing out the occasional speeding ticket, or dealing with a misdemeanor, but let me tell you, he's no Columbo. Or Sherlock Holmes. Or Poirot. I doubt there's a single little gray cell in that noggin of his. He didn't investigate this murder. He let the media police and their talking heads tell him who to arrest."

The monitor beeps grew louder, closer together, and my own pulse began to flutter. "Gram, please calm down. If not for your sake, then for mine."

"I'm fine, child. Good as new. Except for this blasted wrist." She scowled at the cast, then huffed. "Matlock would argue that the only thing that video proves is your mothers didn't like each other."

"Everyone knows that by now." Meg's green eyes were flat with resignation.

Gram cast a piteous gaze on Meg. "I wonder, Meg, if you know that I pegged your mother the first time I laid eyes on her? She was as untamed as a wildflower. She reminded me of your granddad, Daryl Anne. Same restless glint in her eyes. High-spirited. A lust for the unknown. Daniel Blessing was happiest on a boat in some foreign port. Or on the ocean headed for the next adventure. I should never have tried to tie him down, but he had the most irresistible smile."

My mind flashed on a snapshot she kept by her bedside and knew the smile she meant. I had only a vague memory of my dad's father. Very vague. A hearty laugh, a wind-burned face, and strong arms. I knew him better in photos, few as there were.

"The small-town stay-at-home mom wasn't in Tanya's DNA," Billie continued. "She'd fallen in love with a down-to-earth, roots-planted-forever-in-one-place kind of guy. She tried to embrace the life Finn wanted, much as Daniel tried to live in my world, but it was killing her soul. It wasn't what she needed. What she craved. She longed for the next great escapade. She couldn't help it. She was as bound to leave as my Danny was. The hardest, kindest thing she did was to leave you behind with Big Finn."

Meg shifted in the chair, her eyes rounding at the statement, shoulders lifting at the new insight into her mother's abandonment. I prayed perception would lighten the scars on her inner child's heart, even if it couldn't wipe away years of bitter separation. My heart broke a little more for Meg. I reached over and squeezed her hand and held on tight, as much for my sake as hers.

I needed enlightenment too. I struggled to get the words out. "Is what Tanya said true? Would my dad still be alive if Mom had divorced him and he'd left with Tanya?"

Billie frowned. "Where'd you get such a fool idea?"

I relayed the conversation in the restaurant ladies' room with a trembling voice.

"Pish-posh," Billie said. "Meg, I'm sorry, but your mother stretched the truth like it was a rubber band. Daryl loved Susan. And Big Finn was his friend. Oh, there were rumors, but no basis to any of 'em. Probably started by Tanya."

"Then why didn't Mom deny it when she was given the chance?" I didn't want to risk Gram having a setback, but I had to have the answer to the one question that kept digging at me. I wiped my palms on my jeans. "Why did she go after Tanya in the video if she knew it was all lies?"

Billie sank back on the pillows. Her eyelids seemed really heavy now, and I sensed she was struggling to keep them open. The numbers on the monitor calmed. She yawned and then spoke in a low, sleepy tone. "The lies and innuendoes embarrassed and hurt Susan. But she was too shy to stand up against the gossip, which set folks to whispering, 'Where there's smoke, there's fire.' Self-disgust has been building up in Susan all these years. Everyone has a breaking point. After that confrontation at the restaurant, I guess she couldn't hold it in any longer. She must've decided to have it out. Face to face. But Tanya went after her, ripping at her dress, robbing the belt off it like a trophy, showing Susan once again that she was the alpha female."

"Why hasn't Susan told this to the police?" Meg asked.

Billie yawned again, her eyes drifting shut, then popping open. "I suspect she's humiliated that she lost control, and now, thanks to that video, the whole U.S. of A. knows it."

Chapter 17

We hit the jail on the way home but got nowhere with my mother. Despite telling her we knew everything, she wasn't ready to confide in her attorney. I couldn't really blame her. I didn't trust that rookie myself. Meg spent the night again, and I woke the next morning with determination. "We've got to figure out who the killer is, Meg, before my mother ends up living the real *Orange Is the New Black*."

"First, we're going to Cold Feet Café. Peter flew to Texas last night. Ash is dropping Walter at the airport, then driving Peter's Jaguar back to L.A. this morning. I'm meeting her at the café before she leaves. Since I'm staying on a couple of weeks, she'll be filling in for me with the show."

My assistant was doing the same for me.

"Plus," Meg said, "you and I need some fuel or we'll collapse before we can launch our secret investigation."

"Ah, I'm not sure, Meg." Visions of being stared at, pointed at, and gossiped about by people we'd known all our lives enveloped me in reluctance. Meg must have sensed it.

"Oh no, you don't." Meg grabbed my arm as I started to retreat. "If I can face that crowd of locals, so can you."

She was right. Mom and Gram weren't available to hold their heads up, to show the courage of the Blessing family in the face of adversity. But I could. I would. Even if I was quailing inside. We showered and dressed and headed out into the cool May morning. Salty air filled my lungs and boosted my morale. The streets were relatively quiet at this early hour, until we neared Big Finn's. From the looks of it, the breakfast crowd was present and accounted for, digging down.

I hadn't thought I could eat, but the moment we stepped inside the café, the aromas attacked, promising pure delight. I spied Ash in the end booth, perusing an iPad, but I was immediately distracted by a sudden buzz in the collective conversation. My appetite fled.

Ten days ago, Meg and I had been two hometown success stories, everyone eager to welcome us. To celebrate us. Now those same faces were guarded. Suspicious. We'd brought murder to their doorstep. We might even be murderers. Or related to one, in my case. Although I was surprised that Meg wasn't being shown more compassion. Apparently Tanya's outcast status had tainted her daughter. Unfairly.

I bit down an urge to yell at those openly judging us. I took a different tact instead. I donned a bright smile, lifted my chin, and followed Meg. A hand snaked out of the booth ahead of her, catching her wrist. She stopped. I nearly ran into her.

"Hey, good lookin'," Troy said, his voice low and throaty as he gazed up at her with those bedroom eyes. No matter how I hated him for arresting my mother, I had to admit his uniform gave him a certain appeal. If you liked his type. Which Meg obviously did. She sucked in a breath, and I swear I saw her tremble. Yep.

She most definitely had lingering, romantic feelings for the man she was not engaged to.

Meg seemed suddenly aware of staring eyes coming from all directions. She shook free of his grasp. "Good morning, Troy. Seth."

Seth? He peered out from the edge of the booth, his gaze meeting mine, and my pulse seemed to pick up an extra beat as he silently assessed me, asking without words if I was okay. I tilted my head slightly. He grinned that crooked, breath-robbing lift of his sexy mouth. Images and tactile memories of his kiss assaulted me, weakening knees that were already rubbery. But I was still chafing about my mother's arrest, and one way or the other, these two had had a hand in it. "What are you guys up to this morning? Plotting more ways to convict innocent women of crimes they didn't commit?"

Troy raised his hands in surrender. "I had nothing to do with that, Daryl Anne. That was all Sheriff Gooden."

"Blessing, turn it down a notch," Seth said, his voice a low timbre. "We're on your side. Despite the evidence, we know Susan wouldn't kill a fly. We were just trying to figure out how to prove it."

"Really?" The stranglehold of stress loosened around my chest. I reeled in the anger that lay just below the surface. I couldn't guarantee it wouldn't pop up again, and just as quickly, but I realized my emotions were all over the place, that I tended toward reactionary since Mom's arrest and Gram's heart attack.

"Have you found any other leads yet?" I asked in a less volatile tone.

"Not yet, but we aren't giving up." Seth said.

How had I never noticed until returning home what a knight in shining armor Seth Quinlan was? I swear my heart purred just then. "If Mom would just explain herself, tell the sheriff and D.A. why she and Tanya were arguing…"

"Do you mean you know why she and Tanya argued like that?" Troy asked, pulling my gaze from Seth.

Meg answered for me. "She does. Sit down, Daryl Anne, and explain it to them. I have to speak to Ash."

I watched as Meg told the waitress to bring me some coffee and a menu and continued on to the end booth. I joined the two men, choosing to sit beside Seth. I waited until my coffee was delivered along with a sugary cinnamon roll—as if I needed more stimulants—then explained what Billie had told us about how the videotaped fight had come about.

Before I could get another word in, Meg returned to the table, said we had to leave right away, and dragged me out of the booth to the sidewalk. She was as pale as the lone cloud hovering overhead. "What's wrong?"

"Oh my God, you're not going to believe this. I just got an e-mail from someone claiming to know why Peter killed my mother."

I froze, gaping at her. No wonder she was snow-white. *If you say one word about that to Meg, I'll kill you.* Did the e-mailer know the secret Peter was keeping from Meg? The real secret? "Is it the same someone who leaked the video of our mothers' argument at The Last Fling?"

"Yes, and he's threatening to release the information via the same media source."

I frowned, considering this. "I don't get it. What does the e-mailer gain by contacting you? It seems like if he or she had actual proof of motive that Peter would be the one to approach. He'd have the most to lose. He'd be more likely to shell out cash to keep whatever it is hush-hush. Wait. Was money mentioned to suppress the information?"

"No. He claims he's doing me a favor."

"A favor?" More like a back stab. As we started walking away from the café, I was struck by something she kept saying. "Why are you so sure whoever sent the e-mail is a he?"

"Because Ash swears she spotted Kramer in the parking lot of the Happy Hearts motel. Apparently, he's shaved his head and donned heavy, black-framed glasses, but she'd recognize those odd eyes of his anywhere."

They were unforgettable. "So he left and returned?"

"What if he pulled a fast one somehow?"

"But I thought Troy said he sent proof that he was on his way to L.A. at the time of the murder?"

"Was he?" Meg lifted a brow.

"Where are you going with this?"

"We need to find out if he's the one who leaked that video of our moms fighting." She stepped off the curb into the crosswalk with me right at her side.

"You plan on shaking the truth out of him?"

"No, he'll just deny it." She scowled. "Maybe we should get Troy involved."

"He can't search Kramer's car or room without cause."

"Well, then, there's only one thing we can do."

I didn't like the direction her mind was going. As I thought this, I realized we had arrived at Happy Hearts, the same place Meg had been staying three days before the wedding. I rounded on her. "Don't tell me you plan to break into his motel room."

"Of course I do."

"I said don't tell me."

She punched my arm. "How else will we discover what that weasel knows about my mother's murder? He's not going to hand it to us on a silver platter."

Or any other way. I had a bad feeling this wasn't going to end well—as in, Meg and I sharing a cell with Mom. But I found myself trotting eagerly alongside her the same way Seth had followed Sonny. I prayed I wouldn't need rescuing too.

The motel consisted of ten cottage-style cabins set in a horseshoe grid, each separated by a couple of feet, with its own small wooden porch. The doors all bore large red hearts with a number in the center.

"We have a one out of ten chance of guessing his cabin number," I said.

"One out of nine."

"Nine?"

"Ash moved into my cottage when she got here for the bachelorette party. It's still booked in my name. She gave me the key so I can check out."

"Okay. What's the plan then? Are we going to stand around the parking lot or office lobby waiting for someone who might be Kramer to show?"

Meg chuckled. "We're going to go in, and while I'm checking out, we'll finagle some information from the desk clerk, like a cottage number for you know who."

"It might be smarter for you to chat up the desk clerk while I stay out in the parking lot in case you know who shows up," I said, my clear-headed thinking returning like a welcome long-lost friend.

"Ooh, that is better," Meg said. "I'll be right back."

I managed to stand outside the motel office without looking like a vagrant and without spotting Kramer or his doppelganger. Meg was back, grinning slyly, and waggling a hunk of plastic with a brass key hooked to one end. No electronic keys for Happy Hearts. Security be damned. "I thought you were checking out?"

"Not yet. I sort of exchanged keys by mistake. This is to you know who's cabin."

"So no breaking, just entering?" I was sure the police would consider that a minor technicality if we were caught, but why fret about that now? We beelined for cabin 5. I hesitated at the porch. My pulse and my mind were doing the mile-in-a-minute race, leaving me breathless. I might be a willing participant in this crime, but I wasn't a complete idiot. "What if he's in there?"

"Oh. Well, I don't know. We'll say the office gave us the wrong key."

That seemed logical. Didn't it? I held my breath as she opened the door. No big scary man yelled at us. We scrambled inside. The curtains were drawn, and it took a couple of seconds for my eyes to adjust to the dim interior. I was immediately sorry. The décor suggested a piñata full of paper hearts and flowers had exploded, tossing its contents onto every surface.

Meg said, "We need to look for something that verifies it's Kramer staying here."

I headed to the bathroom while she pulled open the closet to check his suitcases.

"Nothing in the medicine cabinet with his name on it," I called. "But there's a razor with a lot of brown hair in the wastebasket."

"Nothing in the closet either," she said with a disappointed tone. "Just a duffel bag with no initials. No camera equipment either."

She'd moved over to the desk as I was exiting the bathroom. I glanced toward the open closet door. Deciding we should leave the room as we'd found it, I went to shut that door, my gaze raking over the few items hanging haphazardly on the cheap metal hangers. My hand stilled, and a first prick of excitement poked me. "Meg, these are the same clothes Kramer was wearing the day we met."

"Really?" I could hear her opening and closing drawers. "He must have his camera stuff with him, either in his car or on his person..." her voice trailed off strangely.

I jerked around to find her peering at an electronic tablet. Light danced across her face indicating movement on the screen. "Did you find the video of Mom and Tanya fighting?"

Her voice had taken on a singsong tone. "This is my mother's tablet."

"Are you sure?" I stepped up next to her.

She pointed to the initials etched into the top. TRJ. "It's the one she carried in her purse."

"No wonder the police couldn't find it."

She turned it on, and it booted up. "Look, there's another video. Oh my God," she laughed. "It's a digital sex tape."

I laughed too, moving toward her. This I had to see for myself. "Like the kind that made Kim Kardashian famous? Kramer doesn't seem like the type who'd record himself in the act."

A gasp escaped Meg, and she recoiled. "No. No. No. No." She shoved the tablet onto the chest of drawers, backing up until her knees struck the edge of the mattress. She dropped to the bed like someone who'd been poleaxed, making a retching noise. Her hand flew to her mouth.

I stepped to the chest of drawers, my gaze glued to the tablet screen. A couple going at it, Foreplay 101. The camera zoomed in on the woman, her mouth over the guy's family jewels. Tanya lifted her head, licking her lips and grinning. The lens went wide angle again, showing her partner. Peter. My stomach turned. My eyes burned as if I'd been standing inches from a blowtorch. "Holy shit."

"I'm gonna be—" Too late. Meg hurled on the bedspread.

I ran to the bathroom, dampened a hand towel, and returned. She snatched it from me, wiping her face and hands. I said, "We have to get out of here."

Meg was trembling. I helped her to her feet. She pulled free and grabbed the tablet, turning it off. "I'm not leaving this here. Kramer might delete it. Or sell it to that online tabloid."

"This doesn't prove that Peter murdered your mother. It only proves they had sex." Why was I being so fair to Peter? Giving him the benefit of the doubt? Probably because I didn't want him railroaded on circumstantial evidence as my mother had been.

"If the date on the file is correct, they hooked up shortly after my mother reached out to connect with me which, at the least, makes him a cheat and makes my mother something even worse."

I had no words. I couldn't imagine what was going through her head. Her fiancé and her mother—ewww. Bile climbed my throat. Oh, sure. Now I was going to vomit.

We heard a car pull into the slot in front of the cottage. Meg hurried to the window. Fear raced through me. She said, "It's Kramer. Is there another way out?"

I grabbed Meg's hand and tugged her into the bathroom.

The window was open.

"It's not big enough," Meg whispered.

"It'll have to be." I hoisted her up, and she squeezed out feet first. Her hair snagged on the latch, and she gave a muted cry. I froze. Kramer entered the cottage, whistling. The main door banged shut. My heart thudded. Meg kept squealing in pain. "Shhhh," I said as I freed her hair.

"Okay, your turn. Hurry."

I stepped onto the commode and maneuvered my upper body through the opening. My heart was pounding so hard I thought it might burst my ribcage and fly out the window before me.

Bedsprings squawked, followed by a yell from Kramer. "What the hell?"

Uh, oh. He'd either spied the puke, smelled it, or sat in it. I hoped it was the latter. With Meg's help, I didn't face plant on the ground beneath the window, but my shimmy over the sill netted me a bunch of slivers. I swear the clatter I made could've awakened the dead. The second I gained solid footing, I was running. I didn't stop to catch my breath. We jogged to the next street over. I slid to a standstill, panting like a racehorse after a derby, my side on fire with pain.

Meg's nose wrinkled, her mouth pursing. "I think I wet my pants."

"I'm sweating too much to tell one way or the other."

"I'm going to be sick again." And she was.

Once we got back to the bridal shop, I did my best to console Meg. But how did you comfort a woman who'd just watched her fiancé boinking her mother? I couldn't get the image out of my head. I couldn't even imagine how much more worse it was for her. Peter was lucky he was somewhere in Texas.

Meg found her phone in the little makeup case she'd used to transform me today. She immediately called Peter, It went to voice mail. She tried calling again and again with the same results, but left only one message, "As soon as you get this, call me."

I hadn't ever had a serious beau. However, I had over the years visualized my ideal man. I was starting to realize that perfect Mr. Right might exist only in my head. Real men were flawed. Imperfect. They made mistakes. They cheated. It was enough to make a woman give up on finding true love.

"Do you think Peter killed my mother?" Meg asked.

"I don't know. But if she was blackmailing him, the tape does give him motive." And now that I knew what Peter was trying to hide, he was my prime suspect. I didn't, however, mention this to Meg. But I would discuss it with Seth the first chance I got.

"Nothing I knew about Peter or Tanya was real," Meg said, sounding lost. "Is it nuts that I just need to hear him tell me himself?"

"No. Not at all."

Meg waited by her cell phone until her eyes were so heavy that she dropped off to sleep. I figured it was for the best. She'd be thinking more clearly in the morning and would know what she wanted to do. I shouldn't have underestimated Kramer. He'd already sold the video to the highest-bidding tabloid. By morning, it had gone viral.

Meg tried Peter the moment we heard the news. The call went straight to voice mail.

He finally called about four hours later. I expected he was using filming as an excuse, but what he said was worse than that. Meg relayed the gist of the call afterward. "He's been on the phone all night and morning with his handlers, coming up with ways to spin this."

I listened, letting her fume, waiting until she choked down some coffee laced with brandy and found her second wind. She set the cup aside, pacing again. "Bottom line is, he lied, even when I gave him the chance to do otherwise. He called his team as soon as he knew the tape had leaked. Not me. I'm not his number-one priority. I never will be."

I was on the edge of my seat. "What did he say to that?"

"He didn't have an answer. Apparently he'll need to meet with his handlers again to figure out how to spin it."

Tears filled her eyes, but the fury issuing off her was palpable. Her shoulders slumped as if she wanted to shrink to invisibility or slip into a closet and hide. "Meg, I'm so sorry."

"No. Don't be. He's finally shown his true colors. I just have really lousy taste in men. Thank God I didn't marry that ass." She glanced down at the huge diamond engagement ring and recoiled. She tugged it off. A strangled laugh slipped from her throat. "He said I could keep it. As if. I might toss it into the sound."

"Use it to start your own salon instead."

She took another hit off the brandy-laced coffee. "He's not the man I thought he was."

No. Sadly, he was the man I thought he was. I kept that to myself. My heart ached for my BFF. She deserved happiness, but he was never the man for her. I hugged her, letting her cry on my shoulder.

Troy showed up to offer his shoulder too, and though I thought his motives were self-serving, I could tell by his gentleness that he cared more about Meg than I gave him credit for. "It's going to take you some time to heal, sweetheart," he told her. "I'll be here for you, if you want me to be."

No pressure. She needed that kind of understanding now. She needed time to grieve the loss of her mother and the loss of the future she'd planned. Time to realize the humiliation of this breakup was not her doing. Or her embarrassment.

As Troy spoke with Meg, I confessed to Seth. "We got into Kramer's cottage at Happy Hearts yesterday and found Tanya's tablet. The police have it now, but Meg and I both saw the video—or at least enough to recognize the participants."

Seth grimaced. "I'm sorry."

"So are we."

Seth said, "According to Troy, there were e-mails between Tanya and Walter Fields. Apparently, she was dating him when she first moved to Hollywood. From what the police have pieced together, she offered Walter a chance to buy the tape. He told her to go to hell. A sex tape might cause an uproar, but it would just boost Peter's fan base."

My eyebrows shot skyward. "How would sleeping with the mother of your fiancée boost your fan base?"

"It wouldn't. Tanya didn't mention she was Meg's mother. Once Walter and Peter learned that, they were more than willing to open their wallets."

"Then they'd have had no reason to kill her."

"It turns out, Tanya didn't just want to be paid off. She wanted Peter to make room for her at the house he and Meg would share, to give her a generous monthly allowance, and to treat her like an adored family member. Or else she'd sell the tape to the highest bidder."

"She was a piece of work," I murmured. "And Peter definitely had motive to kill her."

"As did Walter. Peter is his highest-earning client. Walter's father-in-law wouldn't appreciate a sex scandal touching the agency. I'm sure Walter would do just about anything to prevent that."

"Then the police suspect it was Walter whom Jade spotted in Peter's Jaguar at The Last Fling the night Tanya died?"

"He admits it, swearing that he talked Tanya into being reasonable, since she really did want a relationship with her daughter."

"Ha," I said, feeling as if Meg had been spared a horrible future. "So, if Tanya agreed to make sure the tape never came to light, who killed her?"

"Probably Kramer," Seth said. "He was her co-conspirator,

counting on a slice of the money pie. Tanya betrayed him. Cutting him out completely."

"No honor among thieves." I refilled our coffee mugs. "So he's going to be arrested?"

The look on Seth's face said I wasn't going to like his answer. But before he could respond, Troy strode in, helped himself to a cup of coffee, and joined us at the breakfast bar. "Meg fell asleep."

"We were discussing Kramer," Seth said.

"Can you prove he murdered Tanya?" I asked.

Troy scraped a hand on his bristled chin. "We caught him in a lie. He didn't leave town before the murder because he couldn't book a flight until the next day."

Meg's hunch was right. Kramer had pulled a fast one. "I thought he sent proof that he was on a plane at the time of the murder."

"He said he was sending it, but he didn't," Troy said. Besides, the coroner can't give an exact time of death since the body was in the water for a few hours."

"Then he didn't leave town at all," I said.

"Nope. The murder was making local and national news. He was on the scene and had information no one else did. He figured he'd cash in by selling his stories and videos to the top-paying tabloids."

"Disgusting," I said. "You're going to arrest him, right?"

Troy said, "He's being questioned at the moment."

* * *

While Meg continued to rest, I retreated to alterations to finish the hem on the wedding gown that was being picked up in the morning. The busy work kept me engrossed, so much so that I jumped when the phone rang.

When I saw that the caller was Seth, my anxiety returned in a rush. "Hello?"

I wanted to hear that Kramer had confessed, but Seth said, "I'm sorry, Daryl Anne, but the D.A. feels the evidence against Kramer doesn't prove he's a killer, just a creepy voyeur."

"W-Where does this leave things?"

"They couldn't hold him, but they did tell him not to leave town yet."

I twisted my hands. "Where does that leave my mom?"

"Yeah, well, it turns out that video of Susan and Tanya fighting had been edited. The original was still on Tanya's tablet. It shows her ripping the sash from your mom's dress and tying it around her neck like a trophy. Susan left the bar without it. She'll be released later this afternoon, as soon as the paperwork goes through."

I could've kissed him. Finally, something to smile about. I couldn't wait to tell Meg the news. I thanked Seth and hung up. I set my phone down, extracted myself from the full skirt of the wedding gown, and hurried to the elevator. Then the back doorbell rang.

Chapter 18

I peered through the peephole, relieved that Kramer wasn't standing on my doorstep. I was in too good of a mood just then to let even this guest bring me down. I gave her a big grin. "Hey, Jade. What are you doing here? I thought you'd be on your way to Los Angeles by now."

"Actually, I'm going to Reno as an opening act for a famous country singer." She rattled off the name. "I'm quaking in my boots about meeting him. But I can't leave until I square something with Meg. Big Finn said I could find her here?"

I wasn't sure that Meg was up to company, but she needed to hear my news, and Jade seemed anxious to speak to her too. "She's upstairs."

I led her to the elevator. Once it was moving, she said, "Did Big Finn and Zelda tell her yet about their plans?"

"No, I don't think so. What plans?"

"Oh, nothing. It's better if they tell her." Jade kept wringing her hands, tension oozing from her. "Daryl Anne, it was my brother."

"I beg your pardon?"

"He overheard me talking about how Meg's life was so perfect, whining about how awful mine was, and he thought he was doing me a favor by ruining the wedding tent and drugging Reverend Bell's tea."

"Holy cow."

"I know. I feel so awful. I made him tell the sheriff, and he's going to have to take whatever punishment he has coming, but I wanted Meg to hear the news from me. After what she's done for me, what you did... I can't start my new life with this on my conscience." Jade groaned. "Do you think she can forgive me?"

"Did you or your brother also send me some threatening notes?"

"Notes?" She looked genuinely confused. "No. Absolutely not."

"And you didn't send bachelorette party photos of Meg and Troy to Peter?"

"Hell no." She was shaking her head. "I swear it."

No, I suspected the notes and Instagrammed photos were Tanya's doing. Trying to get me to step aside as maid of honor and to scare Peter. "Then I wouldn't worry about Meg forgiving you. But I have to caution you that she is having a rough time of it. She's called off the engagement in the wake of the video."

Jade gasped. "Oh, man, maybe I shouldn't just drop in. She's got enough to deal with." We'd reached the apartment level. "You can tell her what I said when you think the time is right, and I'll call her at a later date."

"Are you sure?" We exited the elevator into the apartment foyer.

"Positive," Jade said. "I'll take the backstairs and let myself out. I'll be sure the outside door is locked."

"Okay. Thanks." I led her to the stairwell.

Jade took off, and I went in search of Meg, checking my room where she'd been resting. The bed was rumpled, but she wasn't there. "Meg?"

She emerged from the bathroom, dressed, makeup on, and slipping into a jacket. "I want to get out of here for a while. Can we go to lunch?"

"Sure. Why not?"

As we reached the main level, the back doorbell rang again.

"I peered through the peephole, surprised to see the man on the other side. I opened the door. "Walter? I thought you flew back to Los Angeles yesterday."

"No. I spent the day in Seattle with a client. I'm flying tonight."

"Why did you come back to Weddingville then?" Meg asked.

"Ash discovered, my dear, that you'd run off with her phone yesterday at the café. And since you aren't flying back to LA for a few weeks, she asked me to pick it up and bring it with me."

"I'm sorry. I must have thought it was mine. I'm always losing my phone," Meg said. She dug into her purse and pulled out the phone. "You're right. It's not mine."

Instead of handing it over to Walter though, she stared at it, frowning. "Why didn't Ash call me using the phone in the Jaguar and let me know to give it to you?"

"Yeah," I said, gazing at Walter, feeling more uneasy by the second. "Why would you agree to drive this far out of your way just to pick up a cell phone for someone who isn't even a client?"

"Give it to me," Walter said, stepping into the bridal shop and slamming the door.

I froze. "Why do you want Ash's phone?"

Walter seemed to be reining in his temper, trying to calm

down. "Okay, look, the truth is, Ash told me on the way to the airport that she'd gotten a new phone with the capability of file sharing. Just one touch. She loves testing it out. Without asking permission. I'd placed my phone on the table while we had breakfast. Apparently she used the app to transfer sensitive files from my phone to hers. I just want to delete them."

"We could have done that, if you'd called and asked," I said, slowly moving Meg toward the elevator.

"Just give me the phone."

I didn't like his tone. Or the odd glint in his eyes. He was afraid. What exactly had Ash transferred to her phone? Apprehension had me retreating a step. "I don't think we should delete files from Ash's phone without her permission. Why don't we call her now and make sure it's okay?"

"I was hoping you weren't going to make this difficult, ladies." Walter drew a gun from his pocket. "Give me the phone."

Meg threw it at him. As he scrambled to catch the phone, Meg grabbed my arm. "Get in the elevator. Quick."

We ran and scrambled inside. My heart was galloping as I punched the close door button. Hard. The electric door jerked, then began to shut just as Walter appeared between the remaining slit of light. He was lifting the gun.

I yelped. The elevator lurched, then moved.

Bang! The bullet pierced the elevator door and lodged in the back wall. Fear sent Meg and me cowering in the corner. "Why did we run? You gave him the phone. He would've left."

"I gave him my phone." She held up a phone that looked just like hers. "This is Ash's phone. I think we need find out why he's willing to shoot us for these files."

I heard footsteps banging up the backstairs. I leaped up and hit the stop button.

The elevator ground to a halt between floors.

"Good thing we know her password." Meg dialed, then gave the 9-1-1 operator our location and relayed the situation. Instead of holding on as she'd been requested, she hung up and began checking through the files on the phone. "I can't find anything, you look."

I took the phone, praying help would arrive before Walter figured out there was a switch in the electrical panel that would override the manual elevator buttons. A safety feature to prevent anyone getting stuck in the elevator.

I had the same luck as Meg with the files on the phone. I tried the photo gallery next. Sweat beaded my upper lip. An icon caught my attention. I opened it.

Six miniature snapshots. I viewed them one at a time. My stomach did a slow roll. I was staring at death photos of Tanya taken on the edge of a cliff. Only the killer would have these. I quickly e-mailed the photos to Seth along with a cryptic SOS.

The power went off in the elevator. Walter had found the switch. *Jesus.* Meg squealed. I warned her to stay down and got to my feet. Using the phone's light, I located the fire extinguisher. The elevator lurked. Descending. It stopped seconds later. The door began to open. I held my breath, lifting the weapon above my head.

Bang! A bullet whizzed through the opening and grazed Meg's head. She went down. Out cold. Blood seeped from the wound. Fear clawed up my throat and through every fiber of my being. I stayed where I was, the weapon raised. The moment Walter's hand snaked inside, I attacked, slamming the fire extinguisher into his arm and then into his head. He moaned and crumpled.

I went to Meg. She was unconscious. Bleeding. I took off my sweatshirt, pressing it to the wound.

I heard the back door bang open. Then voices. I called, "Here."

Troy and Sheriff Gooden arrived first, guns drawn. Once they realized Walter was no longer a threat, they gathered him up and called in the EMTs. Seth came with them. I'd never been so glad to see him.

He eyed me with concern. "Are you sure you're not injured? You're covered in blood."

I glanced down at my clothes. At the dark stains. "It's Meg's blood," I said, my nerve finally slipping away. I collapsed against him, sobbing. "He shot her, and she's bleeding so bad, and she won't wake up."

Chapter 19

The wedding reception

If nearly dying at the hands of a deranged killer doesn't change your priorities, nothing will. Meg and I were leaving for Los Angeles immediately after the reception broke up. But it didn't seem like that was happening any time soon.

The whole town had turned out to celebrate this wedding, two of their own uniting. Smiles abounded in the reception hall at Tie the Knot. None bigger than on the bride and groom. As the guests looked on, the happy couple took to the floor for the first dance. Jade had been transferred to another agent within the talent agency. She would still be opening in Reno, but she'd stuck around town to offer her vocal services at the reception, feeling like she owed it to Meg. She began singing, and the lyrics—*"Can I have this dance for the rest of my life?"*—filled me with such joy.

But no one was more excited than Meg. "I never thought when we came home for a wedding that it wouldn't be mine."

"Me neither. Are you sorry?"

She considered a moment, then shook her head. "No. Not about them. They belong together. I've never seen my dad like this. I caught him whistling while he was cooking the other morning."

"Zelda is oddly perfect for him."

"She is. And I think she's going to be good for me too."

To see Meg so delighted after dealing with such sadness sent tendrils of joy to my heart.

She'd finally regained consciousness in the hospital to find her father holding her hand, me hovering nearby, and Troy showing up as the case allowed. Six stitches closed the gap in her scalp; the wound was shallow despite the bleeding. The concussion minor.

Troy reported, "At first, Walter claimed he'd talked Tanya into backing off of the demands she was making on Peter, but later he admitted that he'd been lying. Tanya wouldn't listen to reason. She even threatened to send the sex tape to Walter's father-in-law, and that's when Walter lost it."

"But why did he take those photos and then keep them?" I'd asked. "He should have deleted them from his phone."

"Yeah, but he didn't regret killing Tanya," Troy said. "I think the photos gave him a sense of power. Like looking at them made him feel he could do anything and get away with it."

I knew Meg couldn't help thinking that if she hadn't invited her mother to the wedding, Tanya might still be alive, but Tanya had sealed her own fate and, in the end, saved her daughter from marrying an unfaithful man. I hoped one day Meg would accept that and be able to look back on this time without feeling guilty.

"If I hadn't accidentally picked up Ash's phone we might never have known," Meg said.

"And a lot of innocent people would have lived with a cloud of suspicion over their heads. It just proves not all accidents are bad," I said.

For two days following her return to consciousness, Meg had lamented her choice in men, shivering every time she said it. Too much bad news coming in quick succession. But that downward spiral into self-pity and grief ended when Billie told us that Meg's father and Zelda had put their plans to wed on hold when Meg had phoned with the news of her own wedding.

So Meg took matters into her own hands. She'd insisted they marry at once because life was too short to put off joy. The wedding seemed to be the feel-good medicine that the whole town needed.

Jade was midway through the second verse when Troy caught Meg's hand. "Hey gorgeous, we need to cut in on those two and get this party moving."

Meg laughed and let him lead her onto the dance floor. The guests gave a little cheer as Troy swept up Zelda. And as Big Finn gathered his daughter into his arms and twirled her around the floor, a long-forgotten memory came to me of my dad lifting me to dance around the living room when I was very little. My gaze drifted to Mom. She stood near the refreshment table, chatting with a man I hadn't seen before, smiling shyly. Being arrested and sitting in jail, freedom no longer a privilege she could take for granted, seemed to have shaken her out of her staid existence. She got up each morning since her release with an appreciation for the new day, with newfound purpose.

Maybe since Finn had finally opened his heart to love, she was seeing the possibility of that for herself. I know I was. My gaze drifted to Gram, gabbing with her Bunko buddies. No doubt stirring up trouble. Billie seemed to be recovering a little slower.

The wrist, her diabetes, and my leaving seemed to be more than she could deal with and weighed heavily on my heart. Duty and desire, the constant tug-of-war.

"I hear you're leaving today. I'd hoped you'd stay a while longer," Seth said, touching my hair and bringing me around to face him. The longing in his eyes echoed a tremor deep inside me. I'd known better than to encourage these feelings, and yet I hadn't heeded my own advice. The knight-in-shining armor side of his personality lowered my guard and raised my susceptibility to his many other alluring qualities. Like how incredibly desirable he looked in a white dress shirt and gabardine trousers with a camera slung around his neck.

"It's time to start the selection and acquiring process for the wardrobe that will be needed for next season's sitcom episodes." I stared at his mouth, remembering our kiss, longing for so much more than kisses from him. "I'm the only one who knows how to do that."

"I understand," Seth said, his voice giving away the lie. He was too much of a gentleman to contradict me. Or to try and change my mind. He would never keep the lady in his life from pursuing her heart's desire. He was going to make some woman very happy one day. Maybe me.

I decided to stop teasing him and fess up. "I'm going with Meg to return the engagement ring to Peter. A last hoorah to the good life we thought we wanted. Full circle and closure. Peter had Meg fired. With a generous severance package that will allow her to open a salon here on Front Street."

"Wow. That's great."

"It is. And I turned in my resignation. Gram is getting fragile, and Mom can't run the shop alone. Besides, I can't live in Los Angeles without my BFF." *Not to mention, I really want to pursue these feelings between us.* "We'll be packing up our apartment and then head back here in a U-haul."

"Now that is good news." He pulled me onto the dance floor, and I didn't object. He smelled better than wedding cake, felt better than any man I'd ever known. He leaned back, peering down at me, a sexy grin lifting the corners of his mouth. "You stole the bride's thunder in that red dress, Blessing." The glint in his eyes said he wanted to get me out of said garment as soon as possible. "Isn't there a rule against that in the *Maid of Honor's Handbook*?"

"If not, there should be." I found him staring at me with a smoldering gaze. My toes curled as an echoing desire swept through me. Although I was pretty sure of the answer, I asked, "A penny for your thoughts, Quinlan."

He laughed, pulling me closer, whirling me around as he whispered in my ear, "I'm thinking…"

When Quint McCoy returns from a long trip, he discovers his office has been turned into Big Sky Pie—with his soon-to-be-ex, Callee, working at the shop. They soon realize that some couples are so good together that one delectable taste is not enough…

See the next page for an excerpt from

Delectable,

the first book in the Big Sky Pie series.

Chapter 1

I am one sorry son of a bitch, Quint McCoy thought. *A complete, total fuckup.* He didn't have a clue how to rectify the wrong he'd done. It had taken thirty days fishing in the wilds of Alaska, starting in Ketchikan, then deeper inland to the Unuk River, to bring him to his senses. To make him realize he couldn't run from the pain of losing his dad, or from the grief, or the guilt. He couldn't shove it all away. Or cut it out. It would always be inside him, wherever he was—as much a part of him as his black hair and his blue eyes.

Now that he was back in Montana, in the empty house he'd shared with Callee for two short years, he faced another raw truth. He'd bulldozed his life. Leveled every good thing about it. Nothing left for him but to move on and recoup. Somehow.

He grazed the electric razor over the last of the month-old beard, leaving his preferred rough skiff of whiskers on his chin, and slapped on cologne. After four weeks in a small cabin with three other guys, he appreciated the scent of a civilized male. He took note of new lines carved at his mouth and the corners of his eyes, lines that bespoke his misery. *Losing your dad, and then your wife, will do that to you.*

He wasn't proud of the man in the mirror. He didn't know if he ever would be again. He'd trashed his marriage to the only woman he'd ever loved, or probably ever would love. Treated her like the enemy. And worse. Her mother died when she was seven, leaving her to be raised by a taciturn grandmother. She'd grown up feeling unwanted and unloved. He'd made her feel that way all over again. He hated himself for that. If Callee never spoke to him again, he wouldn't blame her.

But then, he wasn't likely to have a chance to speak to her. She'd left his sorry ass, let their lawyers hash out the equitable property settlement, and moved to Seattle right after he told her to divorce him. It took twenty-one days for the paperwork to go through the legal system. By now, he was a free man. And he didn't like it one damned bit.

Quint glanced at the mirror once more, expecting to see *Dumb Shit* stamped on his forehead, but only noticed that he needed a haircut. He pulled on dark-wash jeans, a crisp blue dress shirt and tie, and his favorite Dan Post boots. His dirty clothes went into the duffle on the floor. A scan of the bathroom showed nothing was left behind. He swiped his towel over the sink and counter and stuffed it on top of his laundry, then a second quick perusal, and a nod of satisfaction. Nothing forgotten.

He plunked the tan Stetson onto his still-damp hair and grabbed the duffle. His boot heels thudded on the hardwood floors, echoing through the empty split-level as he strode the hallway, and then down the stairs to the front door.

As he reached the door, his cell phone rang. He snapped it up and looked at the readout. A fellow real estate agent, Dave Vernon. "Hey, Dave."

"Quint. Well, hang me for a hog. 'Bout time you answered your phone. You still in the land of igloos and Eskimos?"

"I wasn't that far north, Dave. But, no, I'm in town."

"Well, now, that is good news. Glad to hear it. How was the fishing?"

"Okay." If the trip had been about the fish, then the fishing was actually great, but it hadn't been about salmon twice as long as his arm. It had been about his inability to deal with the loss of his dad. His inability to stop setting fire to every aspect of his life.

"You still want me to sell your house?"

"That I do."

"Well, as you know, I had it sold…until you decided to skip town. The buyers got tired of waiting for you to return and bought something else."

"I'm sorry, Dave." Although Dave didn't convey it, Quint imagined he was pissed. Quint had cost him a sale. He'd been as irresponsible as a drunken teenager—without the excuse of adolescence. "I'm leaving the house now."

"All the furniture was moved out while you were gone."

"Yeah, I found the note about the storage unit and the key on the kitchen counter." He'd had to crash on the floor in his sleeping bag. "I just picked up the last of my personal items."

"Well, okay, that's good, actually." Relief ran through Dave's words. "I can put this back into the system immediately if you'll swing by and renew the listing agreement."

"Sure. I have to stop at the office first." Quint stepped outside into the overcast day. The end-of-May gloom suited his mood. "Give me an hour or so, and I'll head your way."

"I'm counting on it."

"See you around eleven." Quint stuffed the duffle into the back of his Cadillac SUV and gave the house one last glance before climbing behind the wheel and backing out of the driveway. The development was small, full of similar homes stuffed between Siberian larch and Scotch pine, the kind of place where newlyweds started their futures. *Started their families.* Like he and Callee had hoped to do when they'd moved here.

A heaviness as dense as the cloud cover settled on his heart. He kept his eyes on the road ahead and didn't look back. He didn't need to see the regrets in his rearview mirror; they were etched in his brain. As he drove north toward town on I-93, the vista vast in all directions, he wondered how it could all look so familiar, so unchanged, when he felt so altered.

But something about the crisp Montana air and the wide-open spaces gave him heart. In contrast, the wilds of Alaska—with giant trees pressing toward the river's edge and just a patch of sky overhead—had made him look inward, at acceptance. Here, he could look outward, at possibilities.

Like what, if anything, he might do to salvage his business, McCoy Realty. He knew he'd be lucky if he ever got another listing in this town, but by God, he meant to try. It had taken him three years to build his reputation and clientele list into one of the best in Flathead County, and three months to destroy it. He'd gone from Realtor of the Year two years running to a pariah. The only reason the office was still open was because he owned the building.

And his office manager, Andrea Lovette, hadn't given up on him. Although he'd given her enough reason. Was she at the office yet this morning? He dialed the number, but the female voice that came on the line was electronic. *"I'm sorry, the number you are trying to reach is no longer in service."*

Huh? Had he misdialed? Or had the phones been disconnected? He sighed. One step at a time. Instead of hitting redial, he pulled to the side of the road beneath a billboard and punched in the office number again. Slower this time. The response was the same. He disconnected. One more grizzly to kill.

He tried Andrea's cell phone. The call went straight to voice mail. As he waited to leave a message, his gaze roamed to the billboard. A gigantic image of his own face smiled down at him. An image taken a month before his dad died. Happy times, he'd thought then, not realizing he was already on the track to losing it all. Overworking, ignoring his wife, his mama. His dad. He shook his head. At least this was proof his business on Center Street still existed, sorry as it was. Right across from the Kalispell Center Mall. *Location, location, location.* If nothing else, he had *that* in spades. He supposed it was one positive to hang on to today.

He pulled back into traffic. He needed to confer with Andrea and figure out what steps to take to get the business back on its feet. Starting with getting the phone service reconnected. He called her cell phone again and left another message. Nothing would be easy. He didn't deserve easy.

"Quint, my boy, there isn't a problem so big a man can't solve it with a piece of your mama's sweet cherry pie in one hand and a fishing rod in the other."

Fishing wouldn't solve what ailed him, but a piece of his mama's sweet cherry pie might take the edge off this morning. The thought made his mouth water, but pie for breakfast? Aw, hell, why not? His spirits could use a lift.

His phone rang. He didn't recognize the number. Business as usual for a Realtor. "Quint McCoy."

"Quint," his mother said, warming his heart and his mood. She'd had that effect on him for as far back as he could remember.

"Mama, I was just thinking about you." He'd missed hearing her voice. "How's my best girl? I'm hoping she'll take pity on her poor, homeless son. Maybe do my laundry? I just left the house for the last time, and I'm feeling lower than a rattler's belly. I have some business that can't wait, but—"

"Uh, that's why I'm calling."

"How about I pick you up for lunch and you can tell me how the pie shop is coming?" She was remodeling the half of his building that he wasn't using into a take-out pie shop. It was set to open later that month. The plans he'd seen before leaving for Alaska included a kitchen in back and a display case and counter in front. Small and compact—like his mama. He smiled. "Yeah, that's what I'll do. I'll see you around one, then after lunch, you can give me a tour of your little shop—"

Call-waiting beeped. "Quint, will…please…I—"

He glanced at the phone's screen. A client. *Thank God for small blessings.* "Mama, I have to run. Say, you haven't seen Andrea, have you? She's not answering her cell phone, and I'm hoping to get together with her today. See what we can do to salvage my realty business."

"Well…as—" Call-waiting beeped.

"Look, I gotta take this call, Mama."

"Quint, about Andr—" Call-waiting cut off his mother's words again.

"See you at one," he said, and switched to the incoming call, realizing as he did that some small part of him kept wishing every incoming call would be one from Callee.

* * *

Callee McCoy pulled the small U-Haul truck into the parking spot at the Kalispell Center Mall, cut the engine, and listened to the motor tick-tick as it cooled. One more thing to do. Her hands gripped the steering wheel as though the vehicle careened downhill at uncontrollable speed and an ensuing crash could only be prevented if she hung on tight enough. But the crash had already occurred, rendering her marriage a pile of bent metal and smoking ash, rendering her shell-shocked at the velocity with which the devastation struck.

She felt as someone might who'd been hit by lightning twice—surprised, certain she was immune to any second such occurrence, given the first had been so devastating. Callee thought nothing could ever hurt as much as when her mother died. She'd been wrong. Losing Jimmy McCoy, the only real father she'd ever known, had knocked the pins out from under her again. This time, however, everything should have been different. After all, she had Quint.

A bitter laugh spilled from her, and she gave herself a mental shake. It was all water under the bridge. She was moving on, sadder, but wiser, the Kalispell to-do list almost complete. After landing at Glacier Park International yesterday and renting this U-haul truck, she'd visited the storage unit she'd leased before leaving for Seattle and retrieved the belongings she'd negotiated in the equitable settlement part of the divorce. This morning, she'd met with her attorney, finally given him the go-ahead to file for the final decree, and signed the required paperwork. One loose thread left to tie, and then she was out of here. Montana would be a distant memory that she could look back on whenever she felt maudlin or needed a reminder of how good her new life was.

Live and learn, her mother used to say. Of course, she always said this after bundling Callee out into the night to somewhere her latest disaster of a romance couldn't find them. According to her grandmother, her mother was a tramp. She'd pounded this into Callee's head from the day she came to live with her, hoping, Callee supposed, to make sure that Callee didn't turn out the same. But the mother Callee remembered was a free spirit, always laughing and hugging and promising adventures.

When she was old enough to understand such things, she realized her mother had been acting out, rebelling against a too-strict upbringing by running wild, by living fast and hard as though she knew somehow it would all end too soon. Callee was the end product of both upbringings, as emotionally unequipped for a long-term relationship as a mother who had no idea who'd fathered Callee, and a bitter, taciturn grandmother. As proof, the first punch life threw landed squarely on Callee's chin and knocked her clean out of the ring.

The ring. She glanced at the third finger of her left hand, at the diamond and emerald ring that had belonged to Quint's grandmother. The family heirloom had a fragile, antique beauty, the platinum band filigreed. As much as she adored it, she couldn't keep it. She tugged it off, surprised at the sudden sense of disconnection it brought—as though she'd pulled something of herself loose. Silly. She should have removed it the moment Quint walked out on her.

But she hadn't had the courage to let him go then. Not then. Had she the courage now? Or was shaking Quint McCoy loose from her heart going to be as painful as shaking Montana from her red Dingo boots?

Callee tucked the ring into her coin purse next to a business card, trying to ignore the naked-finger sensation, but knowing it was responsible for her thoughts rolling back to the first time she met Quint. She was in Seattle, about to start cooking school, when she'd received a call that her grandmother had had a severe stroke. Callee flew back to Kalispell immediately, and it soon became apparent that she'd have to sell the house to cover the cost of a nursing home.

Quint represented the buyers. He'd come to present the offer, and one exchanged glance tilted Callee's world. Some might call it love at first sight.

A dinner date led to a kiss; a kiss led to an endless night of lovemaking. She lost her head, her heart, and everything she'd ever meant to be in that conflagration of sensuality. They were like a Johnny Cash/June Carter song—hotter than a pepper sprout, hotter than the flame on Cherries Jubilee, the sizzle and burn an irresistible blue blaze.

Just the memory of those erotic months could melt steel, but then the fire of excitement and sexual discovery calmed to a slow burn. She still craved Quint physically, sexually, but he was so intent on building his real estate business that he no longer had time for her. Somehow, she never got around to telling him that the classes she was about to start just before they met were at a cooking school. Callee feared he might laugh, given she could do little more in a kitchen than boil water. She'd never worked up the nerve to share her secret desire to become a chef or the secret fear that she was incapable of learning to cook.

But the adventurous part of her, which she'd inherited from her mother, was making her try. She'd re-enrolled in that same Seattle culinary college, and her first classes started next week. *Here's hoping the second time is the charm.*

She reached for the truck's door handle and hesitated. She had come to say the toughest good-bye of all…to Molly McCoy. Quint's mother had treated her like the daughter she'd never had and been the closest thing to a real mother since Callie lost her own. Staving off tears, Callee jumped down from the cab into the gloomy day and felt a sudden shiver, like a portent of something dreadful. Probably just her mood. She zipped her jacket and locked the U-Haul.

Her phone vibrated in her pocket, a text from her best friend, Roxanne Nash. Roxy owned a Seattle waterfront bistro, and she'd opened her heart and her home when Callee arrived on her doorstep after leaving Quint. Roxy was always egging Callee on, making her try new things and face her phobia of learning how to cook.

Roxy wanted to know if everything was okay, if Callee was okay, and if she'd started the eleven-hour drive back to western Washington yet. She answered the text, then stepped to the curb at Center Street, her gaze skipping across the road to be caught by a new sign: Big Sky Pie. She knew Molly was renovating the largest part of Quint's office building into a pie shop, but her brows rose at exactly how much of a renovation had occurred.

She smiled, thinking of the treat that awaited Flathead County residents. No one made pies better than Molly McCoy. But it was the example Quint's mother was setting that filled Callee with pride and happiness. Molly had grieved the loss of Jimmy McCoy worse than anyone, yet she'd turned her sorrow into something positive and productive. Callee wanted that end result for herself.

She patted her purse to make sure the ring was still there and hastened across the street, admiring the exterior of the pie shop. Bay windows wore white awnings, and the exterior was painted a rich ruby red with white-and-tan trim and lettering, reminiscent of Molly's specialty, sweet cherry pie made with fresh Bing cherries from the orchards around Flathead Lake. The color scheme was one Callee had suggested when Molly first mentioned she might open a pie shop one day. Callee felt honored that her mother-in-law had remembered and taken the suggestion to heart.

She pasted a smile on her face and tapped on the door, prepared to give Molly an "I love what you've done with the place" greeting. But she startled and then grinned at the woman in the doorway, Andrea Lovette, Quint's longtime office manager and Callee's friend.

Andrea lit up like a delighted child at the sight of a favorite toy. "Oh my God, Callee. I didn't know you were in town. Does Molly know?"

"Not yet, and I'm not staying." They exchanged a quick hug, and then Callee stepped back and looked at her friend. "I'd ask how you're doing, but you look fabulous."

"I look ragged. Two little boys will do that to you." Andrea laughed, her brown eyes sparkling as she shoved at her long, thick blond hair. She was taller than Callee, a fact made more pronounced by the skinny jeans and platform pumps she wore. "Since you're not staying, what brings you back to Kalispell?"

"Tying up some loose ends."

Andrea nodded, her lips pressed together. "Well, whatever the reason, I'm delighted to see you. And Molly will be, too. Besides, I hate being the only guinea pig."

Guinea pig? Callee found herself being pulled farther into the shop. "I don't know what you're talking about. Where's Molly?"

"In the kitchen with Rafe, her new assistant pastry chef. She's teaching him something, I think."

Muffled voices issued from the kitchen, one female speaking English and one male speaking Spanish. Callee smiled. "Do they even understand each other?"

"No clue, but Molly will be out in a minute. I'm sitting over there." Andrea pointed to a booth. "Go ahead. Sit. I'll bring you some coffee."

"Okay, but I can't stay long." Only long enough to give Molly the ring and a hug good-bye. Callee settled into the booth and began to take in the décor. The interior reflected the colors used outside, but in reverse. The walls were tan, the crown molding and trim white, and the tablecloths and napkins a ripe red. This was all café, display cases, cash register, and an espresso/coffee and tea counter. Seating consisted of a row of four high-backed booths on one wall and round tables scattered throughout the space.

"Isn't it great?" Andrea handed her a cup of steaming coffee. "The kitchen consumes the largest portion of this building, an L-shaped chunk that isn't visible from this room."

"It's wonderful. Right down to the framed, poster-sized photos of juicy pies with sugar-coated crusts."

"Mouth-watering, huh?" Andrea took a sip of coffee.

"That's the idea, right?" Callee couldn't get over the size of the room. "I didn't know she was going to do a café. Last I heard, the pie shop would be take-out only."

"Yeah, well, the café was kind of last minute," Andrea said, quickly downing more coffee. "Molly told me the design was yours."

Callee shook her head. "Nope. Only the colors."

"All the same, I think you missed your calling, lady."

Callee smiled. "I missed a lot of things."

"So, how are you doing?" Andrea touched her hand.

The gesture made Callee feel less alone. Andrea had once been where she was now, figuring out how to be single again. The difference was that Andrea had had the burden of two little boys relying on her to get it right. Callee had only herself. *Thank God.* "I'm looking forward, not backward."

"I'm glad. I've been worried about you." Andrea offered a commiserating smile.

"I promise, I'll be okay, eventually." She smiled weakly.

"This whole thing is such a tragedy." Andrea shook her head, but never one to hold back how she was feeling, she added, "When Quint comes to his senses, he's going to be real damned sorry. I wish you'd stick around, Callee. I know he said and did some awful things, but that man loves you. Even if he can't see past his grief right now."

"If that's what he thinks love is, I want no part of it." It didn't matter if he did love her, or even if she still harbored tender feelings for him. He was, after all, her first true love, but she had never been a priority with him, and watching the love his parents had shared, she realized she deserved better than what Quint was giving. One day, maybe she'd find her Mr. Right. But Quint McCoy was not that man. "My U-Haul is parked right across the street. As soon as I have a minute with Molly, I'm on my way to Seattle. I've enrolled in college," she said, keeping the type of college to herself. If she ended up with her degree then she would share details with trusted friends, but for now, it was her secret. "Classes start next week."

"That's awesome. I'm so excited for you." Andrea's smile flashed, then quickly faded. "Uh, by the way, Molly just spoke to Quint. He's on his way here."

"What? I thought he was still in Alaska." The news tweaked Callee's nerves, and she gulped down a swallow of coffee, the hot liquid burning its way to her stomach.

Andrea was studying her. "He got back last night."

Callee set her mug aside, snatched hold of her purse, and scooted toward the end of the banquette. "It's been wonderful visiting with you, but right now, I need to see Molly and get out of here."

"Okay, Andrea, I hope you're hungry," Molly called, emerging from the kitchen. Quint's mother, a bubbly, middle-aged redhead with short spiky hair, was followed by a tall, handsome Latino in his early twenties, who carried a serving tray with fragrant goodies on dessert plates.

"Callee!" Molly squealed, foiling Callee's attempted escape. Molly wiped her hands on an apron spotted with flour, chocolate, and fruit juice and hugged Callee. "Oh my God, you're like a gift from Heaven."

Callee returned the hug, wishing she never had to let go, but she did, and since the memory of this moment would have to last her a long time, she held on a beat or two longer than she might have. Even though Molly would always welcome Callee into her home and her heart, Callee understood their relationship would never be the same once she left here today. Tears stung her eyes.

Molly stepped back, and Callee did a quick assessment. There was a smidge of flour in her choppy red hair and on her pert nose. The bedroom eyes she'd passed on to her son seemed weary, and the wide smile that lit up any room she entered seemed less brilliant. She was like a clock someone forgot to wind; not quite up to speed. Still missing her husband, Callee figured, still worrying about her son. At least the shop would joyfully fill a lot of lonely hours.

Callee glanced at the wall clock, wondering how soon before Quint arrived. She had to leave. Now. But Molly urged her back into the booth.

"I know why you're here."

How could she know that? Callee lowered her voice. "In that case, could I see you in private—?"

"You're going to stay and come work for me." Molly cut her off, hope erasing the worry lines near her mouth.

"What?" Callee's eyebrows rose. "Work for you doing what?"

"A pie shop can always use more than one pastry chef." She handed Andrea and Callee forks and napkins.

"A pastry chef?" Callee blushed, recalling the time Molly tried to teach her to bake a pie. Callee kept hearing her grandmother's voice, taunting, telling her that she was only fit for washing dishes and taking out garbage. Not for cooking or baking anything. The end result had been a crust that resembled lumpy clay, and although Molly had been kind, Callee couldn't stop cringing at the memory.

Callee gave Molly an indulgent smile. "You know perfectly well that my kitchen skills are limited to coffee and scrambled eggs. Period. Not pies."

"Oh, all right." Molly sighed. "But since you don't have anything against *eating* pies, you can help us figure out which of these three items belongs on the menu."

"I really need to go."

"I'm opening next week, and I need to tick this off my to-do list."

"I can't st—"

"Nonsense. It'll only take a few minutes." Molly slipped into her side of the booth, blocking her in. As stuck as gum in cat fur, her grandmother was fond of saying. Resigned, Callee turned her attention to the tray, which held three colorful pie slices. Her mouth watered. Her early morning breakfast had consisted of a grande latte. Eating something now meant one less stop along the road later on.

Andrea said, "If presentation means anything…wow."

Molly beamed. She handed Andrea a small green tart. "It's key lime."

Molly gave Callee a slice of chocolate pie and gestured for Callee to try it. "This is tar heel pie."

Callee tried a bite. "I've never heard of it."

"It's chocolate chips, coconut, and pecans. A word of caution. It's very rich and should probably only be eaten in tiny increments."

"Ooh, I like this," Andrea said. "A definite ten."

"This is to die for," Callee exclaimed, her sweet meter tilting off the charts. She shoved the slice toward Andrea. "Try it."

Molly pointed to the next item. "This last one is Daiquiri pie. Cream cheese, condensed milk, concentrated lemonade, and my own twist, ninety-proof rum."

Andrea and Callee dug in while Molly watched, waiting for their verdicts.

But Callee and Andrea could only moan in pleasure.

Molly glanced at Rafe. "So much for narrowing the menu."

He muttered something in Spanish that sounded like "a bucket of Tequila" and headed back to the kitchen.

Outside, tires crunched on the gravel parking lot. Inside, forks stopped halfway to mouths. The three women exchanged knowing looks. Molly scooted out of the booth, then stood frozen beside the table. "Quick, Callee, go see if it's Quint."

"Me? Why me? I don't want to see Quint." She would just mail the ring to Molly. Feeling none too composed, Callee slipped from the booth. "Do you have a back door?"

"Please, Callee." Molly's face had gone a worrisome gray.

"What's going on?" Callee looked from Molly to Andrea.

Andrea winced. "A sort of intervention."

"Shock therapy," Molly said.

"What?" Callee had no clue what they were talking about, and she didn't want to know. She stole to the window and peered out through the blinds. The second she saw Quint, her heart began to thrum with a rhythm akin to a love song. He was sitting in his SUV, phone to ear. "It's him."

"It's for his own good," Molly muttered, as though to herself, as though her actions needed defending. "It's true what they say about tough love. It is harder on the giver than on the receiver. If I hadn't spoiled that boy to the edge of redemption..."

"What's he doing?" Andrea asked, still seated in the booth, sucking up Daiquiri pie like she was downing shots in a bar and ignoring her cell phone, which kept announcing a new voice mail.

Callee had a bad feeling. "He's putting his phone away."

"What's he doing now?" Molly asked, her face drained of color.

"Getting out of the car."

"Does he look angry?" Molly asked.

He looks heart-stopping delectable—like always. Damn. Callee hated that her pulse still skipped whenever she laid eyes on Quint, hated that every nerve in her body seemed to quiver as he shoved back the Stetson revealing his incredible face. God, how she adored that face. His smile, his touch, the things he did to her body, the responses he elicited... just recalling left her breathless. *No. Stop it. You're over. He never put you first. Never.* "He's glancing up and down the street as though he can't understand why he isn't seeing what he expects to see."

"Like he's wondering if he's on the right street?" Andrea said, sounding... anxious?

And then Callee realized. *Shock therapy.* "You didn't tell him you were turning his office into the café portion of your pie shop?"

Molly gulped. All the answer Callee needed. Before she could ask what the hell Molly was thinking, a fist hit the door. All three women jumped. But no one moved to let him in.

About the Author

Adrianne Lee lives with her husband of many, many years on the beautiful Olympic Peninsula in Washington State in a pole barn building her husband transformed into an upstairs apartment with a shop below for his hot rods. Adrianne creates her stories on her laptop, in her recliner with her adopted cat, Spooky, curled between her calves, snoozing. More than thirty years of summer vacationing in the Flat Head Lake area near Kalispell and Glacier Park have given her a love for all things Montana.

FOREVER

Don't Miss Any of the Books in the Big Sky Pie Series

by Adrianne Lee

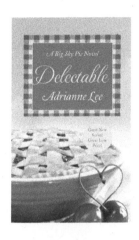

You Might Also Like...

Can a secret crush...

Jo Walsh has loved Cameron Mitchell for as long as she can remember. Whether front and center in her life or on the periphery, the tall, brooding artist has made his presence seductively and irresistibly known. But whenever they start to get close,

Cam pulls away. Jo's tired of keeping her feelings in a box Cam is afraid to open. If he wants her, he'll have to prove it. And if he doesn't, Jo will need to know the *real* reason why...

...*become the love of a lifetime?*

How do you walk away from your soul mate? Cam wishes he knew. No matter how far he runs from Jo, he can't resist looking back at the silver eyes that seem to see right through him. But as well as Jo thinks she understands Cam, the dark truth about his past is something she shouldn't have to handle. Cam's sure that setting Jo free is the right thing to do. Too bad his heart has other ideas...

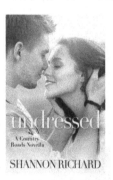

She knows the rules of the game... but she can't resist his moves

Publicist Abby Fields's career is on the rise. And with failed romances in her past, she has no time for men. When a job opportunity opens up with a sports team in Florida, Abby eagerly packs up and heads south. Yet after a work event in Mirabelle, Florida, Abby finds herself in the arms of a hockey player whose heart-stopping smile leads her to the steamiest night of her life…

Logan James is hot on and off the ice. With his team on an epic winning streak, life couldn't get better…until he meets Abby, the fiery redhead assigned to protect his team's image. Now Logan's finding it difficult to concentrate on anything other than getting Abby undressed. But after a secret is leaked to the press, the taste of betrayal opens old wounds. If they can't learn to trust each other, they may risk losing more than their hearts.

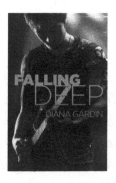

Reed Hopewell is a lot of things
to a lot of people…

To his parents, he's the son who needs to get serious. To his friends, he's the player they all want to be. And to his fans, he's the hottest rocker in Charleston. But never has Reed been anyone's hero—until the night he finds Hope.

Hope Dawson can count the number of men she trusts on one hand. Definitely not the guys she goes out with or the stepfather who treats her like property. She'd be out of his house tomorrow if not for the need to protect her little sister. But when things at home go from bad to worse, Hope has to act fast—and Reed is the only person she can turn to...

When life gets tough and love is hard to find,
four friends take their troubles to lunch. High school
teacher Danielle Bradshaw deserves a happily ever
after, and the Ladies Who Lunch are determined
to deliver Mr. Right.

HOT FOR TEACHER

As the new head of the English department, Dani doesn't have much time for anything but lesson planning and literature. Romance—or even sex? Forget about it. But then the principal introduces her to last-minute hire Nate Ryan. Finding time to mentor a new teacher won't be easy, especially when his incredible body and equally disarming charisma are enough to make her heart skip a beat...

Nate may be fresh out of school, but he's confident in his teaching skills—and in his feelings for Dani. But while she's everything he's ever wanted, he knows his place on her staff—and his age—may be problematic for his sexy boss. How can he convince her to ignore the gossip mill currently in full swing in the teacher's lounge and surrender to what's meant to be?